W9-CJX-833

FUNNY, JONAS,

YOU DON'T LOOK DEAD

By Mary McMullen

FUNNY, JONAS,
YOU DON'T LOOK DEAD

MARY McMULLEN

PUBLISHED FOR THE CRIME CLUB BY

DOUBLEDAY & COMPANY, INC.

GARDEN CITY, NEW YORK

1976

All of the characters in this book
are fictitious, and any resemblance
to actual persons, living or dead,
is purely coincidental.

Library of Congress Cataloging in Publication Data
McMullen, Mary, 1920–
    Funny, Jonas, you dont look dead.

    I. Title.
PZ4.M168Fu   [PS3563.A31898]   813'.5'4
ISBN: 0-385-11415-x
Library of Congress Catalog Card Number 76-2797

To A. H. Montmorency

FUNNY, JONAS,

YOU DON'T LOOK DEAD

One

"No, Jonas," Millie mumbled to the ringing of the telephone. "Absolutely not."

It was—she blinked at the bedside clock—ten minutes to one on what would have been their fifth wedding anniversary.

She had spent a fourteen-hour day at her drawing board, working against an impossible deadline and meeting it. The telephone snatched her from a sleep miles deep.

Jonas always called her on June the second, late or early, depending on how you defined time. He was one of the world's telephoners and was perfectly capable of going on for thirty minutes, forty, an hour.

". . . No, don't hang up yet, Millie, sweet. Remember that afternoon in Nantucket, at Jetties Beach? When the couple under the yellow umbrella got out their guitars and in ten minutes the whole beach was singing? God, how I wished I'd had a movie camera! Wasn't it fun, that summer, Millie . . . ?"

Jonas by no means accepted her view that as far as emotional involvement was concerned he was a closed book.

Incurably festive and friendly, he sent her armloads of flowers on her birthday, lavish presents at Christmas. He kept her informed of his whereabouts—San Francisco, New York again, Philadelphia now. He asked her advice about which job to take, which to reject. In turn he offered his counsel to her.

"How much did you get for that television job, the opening and closing billboards for Comet Mills? Twenty-five hundred? You're mad, girl. Anyone else would have gotten double. . . ."

Thanks to him, she had half-mastered the difficult art of not answering the telephone at unlikely hours of the night. If the call was really important, whoever it was would reach you the next day, anyway. If it was not, you were saved a good deal of boredom and fuss and a broken sleep.

The ringing had stopped, but it had set up a steady beat of pain in her head. Sighing, she got out of bed and went into the bathroom and took two aspirin.

They had been married for three years, divorced for two. An uncomplicated divorce: Jonas had left her and gone to that girl, that particular girl of that time, in Boston; he had made it clear that there was no longer any point in his coming back.

She had a feeling the anniversary call was not shelved. Lying on her side, willing sleep to come and swallow her, she watched the telephone with wide-open eyes, and sensed it gathering itself to give voice. The second it started to ring, she snatched it up. Oh, God, get it over with, this could go on all night.

"Just got in, Millie?" His buoyant voice was a little softened and blurred, perhaps with champagne, which he told her he always drank on their anniversaries. "I tried before, no answer. Had to call, sweet, couldn't not— Are you there?"

"Yes, Jonas, and it's late and I'm tired."

She couldn't at all manage to stand beside him and read his script with him. Jolly friends, parted lovers, the past merrily dismissed, and now her role as Jonas's dear familiar Millie, an anchor of sorts, a bedrock.

"Don't sound cross, it's not like you—my beautiful mannerly Millie. Can't we take a few minutes to light a candle together? It was pretty damned wonderful in places, you must admit. Our only problem is that you're as constant as the moon, and I was and still am—well, you know about that. . . ."

For the moment, she could find nothing whatever to say. She sat on the edge of the bed, shivering a little in the cool night wind. Ridiculous to feel guilty about being unable to respond to his warmth, guilty about turning her back to something that had to have a firm back turned against it, for pride, for survival, for ordinary everyday living and breathing.

Wearily, she got out a "How's the job, Jonas, do you like it?"

"Terrific, the best racket I've stumbled on yet—" And then an over-the-shoulder tone of voice—someone must be in the room with him, wherever he was—"I suppose you think I'm kidding. Great old kidder, Jonas is—" on an edge of laughter.

"But," Jonas said, his voice firmly redirected to her, "enough of pleasantries. Let's get down to business, Mr. Farnall." A different voice, crisp, a little formal. "I don't like to trouble you at this hour, but I think when you hear what I have to say you'll be—"

The sounds that followed happened almost simultaneously, but later she was able to separate and ticket them.

A thundering, crashing noise with an echoing hard, whistling ring at its core.

A strangled screaming.

An unspeakable gurgle.

A small dim thump, hollow.

The first, gunshot, still reverberating in some faraway room, or was it in her own body—?

The second sounds, Jonas wounded—Jonas dying? Dying on the telephone?

The third, the receiver escaping a dangling hand, smacking the floor.

It was strange that in that paralyzed moment or two she was so nakedly sure of what she was hearing. Unmistakable in its savagery and finality.

Later, the doubts and confusions flooded in. Thunder, a backfiring car or truck, a slammed door, a huge dropped object, a champagne cork popping, a ceiling falling down. The scream, the gurgle, merely indicating shock or violent surprise. Or mock acting of some kind, Jonas putting on a show.

But at one twenty-five on the morning of June second, Millie was sure she had heard her ex husband shot.

With it came the feeling, irrational, inseparable, that by not answering earlier, the first time, she had interfered with some intricate machinery, and that she herself had had a hand in the shooting of Jonas.

One part of her mind telling her that this was stupid, hopeless, she called into the phone, "Jonas. *Jonas*." Again and again. "Jonas, are you there? Jonas, please . . ." Tears were running down her face. She heard herself shouting. "*Jonas—*"

The line was still open. There was a heavy untidy toppling sound. A small neat click as the receiver was replaced. And then the low steady buzz. The telephone call was over.

In the next few minutes she got an unearthly taste of the fragility of her own sanity. Weeping, shaking, striding the darkness of her apartment, gripping her hands together, wringing them, clutching at herself to hold herself together, keep from flying apart and splashing off the walls, hearing some breathless frantic voice calling, "Jonas, Jonas . . ."

Then she drew back from a dangerous yawning edge. She took a tremendous breath and dropped her hands to her sides. She turned on all the lights in the apartment, the bedroom, the studio-living room, the bathroom, the kitchen. She summoned reality from the tossed blue-and-white flowered sheets on the bed, the finished work stacked on the table beside her drawing board, the innocent white plastic of the telephone.

Now, begin at the beginning. Jonas is in Philadelphia. Some kind of accident may have happened while he was calling. (Already, the softening and blurring of what had been so sharp and terrible—the might's and perhaps's and maybe's.)

Police. Philadelphia police. "Please get me the Philadelphia police, Operator, a life or death matter." Official male voice, "Just a moment, madam." And then the half-gasped information from her end, accompanied by a sinking feeling that they would have every reason to think she was drunk, or crazy, or both.

"I was just talking to a man—he was my husband—and I think somebody shot him—"

"Yes, ma'am. If you were talking to him you would have *seen* someone shooting him?" patiently.

"No, I mean, talking on the telephone. I'm in New York, but he's there in Philadelphia. I realize it's very late, but I'm sure the sound—"

Probably to get her off the line, a tired request for her husband's home address; a patrol car would be sent.

"But I don't know whether he was at home or where he was, but yes, just a minute—"

A wild search for the address book.

"Delancey Street . . . wait, here's the number. He said, I think, I'm not sure, it's the top floor apartment. There's a side or back entrance, a flight of stairs—"

Name, please, of her husband. Age. Description.

She would be called back when the patrol car had checked out the apartment. Accident cases and fatalities reported from Philadelphia hospitals would also be checked. And then, surprisingly, "Relax, he's probably just out on the town and someone broke a bottle or something . . ."

She made coffee, drank it hot and black, and waited, hearing sirens screaming, feet thundering up Jonas's stairway, a shoulder crashing against a locked door or, yes, of course, they'd have a way of opening locked doors, wouldn't they? Jonas face down, blood . . . silent.

She had lost valuable minutes, roaming the apartment in the dark, crying his name. If she had called instantly, perhaps he would be alive. How long had she held off help for him? Sixty seconds? Ten minutes? She had no idea.

Exactly fifteen minutes after her call, a young, nice voice:

"Apartment's in order. Nobody there, no sign of a struggle. Looks pretty peaceful. If he turns up at a hospital we'll let you know."

Turns up. Like a piece of merchandise. "Thank you officer, I do appreciate it. It may be nothing at all."

Jonas, now, may be nothing at all.

Or, yes, let's say he was out on the town. He was an inveterate partygoer and as far as she knew hadn't changed his ways. A night man, inexhaustible. "We're having too much fun to pack up now. Just one more drink—and then there's that place down the street where the bartender juggles five hardboiled eggs at once while he sings dirty songs in Russian—" The man at police headquarters, and her own second guesses, were, she told herself, probably right.

At any minute he would climb his stairs, shed his clothes, wander into the kitchen for a nightcap, brush his teeth—Jonas had never been known to go to bed, no matter what the hour, without brushing his teeth—reach for a book he wouldn't read and then tumble instantly into sleep.

It would be only fair for the telephone to return the comfort, the status quo, it had taken away from her. She dialed his number, with an obsessive calm and determination, every fifteen minutes from shortly after two o'clock until after three, when the telephone was answered.

Two

Hearing the ringing at the other end abruptly interrupted, she very nearly fainted with relief.

A male voice, baritone, trying without much success to conceal rage.

"For God's sake who's this?"

"Is . . ." trying to get her breath back, "Jonas there, please?"

"No, he is not. I sleep on the floor beneath, and this phone has been going for one solid hour and I couldn't stand it any more. Would you, whoever you are, mind letting whatever this is go until morning?"

Millie burst into tears.

Through her own exhausted, wet noises she heard him say, after a pause, "Look, if you're one of his girls, you know he's given to late nights. I'll take a message for him if you like," with distaste in his voice at the sobbing, and a touch of startled sympathy.

She made a great effort to control herself. If he slept on the floor underneath, this must be Jonas's landlord. Jonas had said something about him in his birthday letter. . . . The art director at his agency happened to have an empty apartment at the top of his house, which he thought would suit him nicely.

If she could manage to sound halfway sane, he might be helpful.

"I'm sorry about the commotion. I'm Millie Lester, I used to be married to Jonas. He called me because this is, was, our anniversary and there were awful sounds in the middle of the call, and I thought—" gather your strength, this does sound mad—"that he'd been shot, maybe killed. I'm in New York—"

Silence. She could see him staring at the telephone and thinking, What on earth have I got on the other end of this line?

"I've called the police, they've been there; this was an hour or so ago. I thought he might have come in in the meantime."

"Well, he hasn't. I came in late myself, as a matter of fact I passed the police car a few doors from the house—" In the cheerfully calm voice useful for dealing with irrational people, he went on, "Sedate as it's supposed to be, this can be a hell of a noisy town. There are all sorts of explanations for frightening sound effects."

"Sedate as you're supposed to be, you have a very high crime rate," she said crisply. "And I've been through the backfiring trucks and local thunderstorms and champagne corks, and they don't quite fit."

Another pause. Probably wondering how he was to get rid of mad Millie Lester and get back to bed.

"You've put it in the hands of the police, there's nothing more to be done at the moment. He'll probably turn up here by morning. If not—he and I work at the same place, but he comes and goes at odd hours. Say he doesn't show up for a couple of days—I'll let you know, will I?"

A most soothing and sensible way of looking at things. Let the smoke clear, and then see if there was really anything it was hiding from the eye. Give it a couple of days, not this minute-to-minute touching elbows with hysteria.

"Yes, please. Here's my number . . . and thank you. I hope you manage some sleep, Mr. . . . ."

"Welcome. Augustus Welcome. Good night—I assume you're Ms. —Lester? I'm sure you have nothing to worry about. I don't know Jonas as well as you do, but he seems to have a way of landing on his feet."

In spite of the sounds in her head, repeating themselves in a kind of deadly lullaby, she got into bed at three and slept until after nine, trying to adopt Augustus Welcome's wait-and-see policy.

He called at ten. "I didn't want to keep you hanging. . . . No, Jonas didn't turn up after all, but—"

"Yes, I know. Unattached men don't always sleep at home."

His voice, with the late-night rage gone out of it, was extraordinarily pleasant to the ear, and in some way comforting.

"There's a meeting here he should be at, at three. But his skipping it unfortunately won't prove anything. . . ."

Jonas up to his old tricks, she thought, a talented but unreliable pair of hands. (Millie, it doesn't do to toe the line. Only drones turn up exactly when expected; absence makes the heart grow fonder.)

As if dipping his toe in water that might be too hot, he asked carefully, "Now in broad daylight, you don't still think—?"

A stranger. She had no right to dump her waking nightmare on him.

"As you said, it's in the hands of the police. Thank you very much for calling me."

"I don't like you sounding so dead calm after the tears and the panic," the stranger said. "Are you all right?"

"Yes, I'm all right. Sorry—my cleaning woman's at the door—"

Ordinarily, she fled the apartment when Rose came. She had never gotten over a slight guilt, discomfort, at the sight of another woman on her hands and knees, scouring and scrubbing for her.

But today she was condemned to stay with her terrifying companion, the telephone.

However, it could serve as well as attack her. After she had summoned a messenger service to deliver yesterday's—*yesterday's?*—work, she began calling New York friends and acquaintances of Jonas's. Gregarious and effortlessly likable, he had a lot of them. She got it down to a simple formula: Hello, I'm in a hurry, hunting Jonas, have you talked to him?

Nobody had, not this past week. A mutual friend, Belle Verelli, was the only one who refused to let her slide quickly off the line and get on to the next call.

"Millie, what's this? What do you want with Jonas? After what he did to you—you're not retrogressing?"

"No, it's just that I heard he was in some kind of trouble." She couldn't bear to go into the night's tale, bring it back whole and real and live it again, with Belle.

"He's often in some kind of trouble, mostly self-created. Be honest, Millie, you're not still a little in love with him?"

"No—"

Too complicated and time-consuming, now, to say what she felt about Jonas. She had an exasperated fondness for him, and a kind of family feeling that had nothing to do with her heart and her body. She had concluded some time ago that what had happened between them was pleasure, passion, and amusement, and that there hadn't really been love, at all. Otherwise, wouldn't there be some deep, enduring pain at losing him, some wound that hadn't yet and never would quite heal?

But people couldn't be allowed to go around shooting other people. And what sort of unspeakable pain had his scream been describing . . . ?

"I'll call and talk when I have time, Belle."

"Millie, you sound frightful. Shall I come around?"

"No, I have a million things to do."

What million things? What would be constructive, sensible to do right this minute?

Mike Garland couldn't be turned to for help, for comfort. He had left several days before to shoot three television commercials in Rome, and said he expected to be away for at least a week. Liberation notwithstanding, it would be terribly nice to have a man around, saying firmly, Pack of nonsense, Millie, you have an overripe imagination. But if it will make you feel better, we'll go and have a quick look around. . . .

She took a fast ten minutes from her vigil at the apartment to go out and get a Philadelphia *Inquirer*. West Eleventh Street looked as if nothing out of the ordinary had happened; sunlit, calm, its trees dropping circles of shadow almost black in the dry brilliant light.

The *Inquirer* was studded with horrible small paragraphs: an unidentified man, dead three days, found in an abandoned car in Fairmount Park; a dead baby in a box; deaths by fire, stabbing, drowning; deaths in the center city, the black ghettos, the suburbs.

If there was anything about Jonas, what would it say? "Found shot to death, a man identified as Jonas Rath, 35, of Delancey Street. Rath was a consultant to the advertising firm of Homans, Inc., on Walnut Street. The body was found . . ." Where?

She realized with devastating clarity that the Philadelphia police wouldn't, couldn't, take the matter of Jonas very seriously and doggedly pursue it to a conclusion. A crazy call from a gasping woman in New York, babbling about sounds heard over the telephone, a gnat to be brushed away when there was visible violent crime to be dealt with hourly.

Puzzle over your own mysteries, Ms. Lester. We are far too busy for guessing games.

Guessing games. Why had he addressed her as Mr. Farnall? Was there something, someone in their past he was teasing her about, named Farnall? Or, it could have been Farnold, or Farnham. . . . She thought hard and could find no echo of the name. Jonas had always been better at names than she was.

With the apartment breathing cleanliness, Rose left at four. "We're almost out of scouring powder, and I could use a new mop. You look tired. Why don't you take a nice nap? If you've finished with the *Inquirer*, I'll take it along. I have a sister in North Philly."

She found herself, alone now, hesitating, over a deep inner trembling that hadn't gone away all day.

Let it drift? Let it go?

She was, after all, his yesterday. He was in no sense her responsibility.

There would be people in his present who would be wanting his company, for lunch, for laughter, for drinks, for love. They'd be hunting him, calling around. They'd know his habits and his habitats.

Let them take on the fearful unexplained. Let them probe possible disaster.

Against her will, she saw the sweet innocence of Jonas's sleeping face. Heard his laughter, a catching sound that made even strangers smile. Listened to him saying, "Millie darling, you're the *dearest* girl I've ever been unfaithful to. . . . Forgive me, do. . . . Let's go out and come in at another door and start again. I promise you that, this time . . ."

She called Information, renamed Directory Assistance, and reached Augustus Welcome at Homans.

"Sorry to keep bothering you—I think now I ought to come to Philadelphia tomorrow, and will you let me have a key to Jonas's apartment? There are all sorts of things—for instance, I can tell from his bags if he went away overnight somewhere. And then I can go to the police myself and try to convince them they're dealing with a normal woman and not a nut from out of town, and that something really did happen, last night—"

"Of course you can have the key," he said. "Tell me what train, and I'll hand it over to you at the station."

"You don't have to do that—"

"It's no trouble. I'm only a few blocks away from Thirtieth Street. What do you look like? Although in a way I think I'll be able to recognize you—"

She had, without being exactly aware of it, a delightful voice, soft and thrushy, which courted the ear with its natural music.

"A little sleepless—I'll be wearing," she thought a moment, "a blue linen suit and carrying a white canvas bag with leather corners, suitcase I mean. What do you look like?"

"I'll be right at the top of the escalator, if it isn't broken, or at your stairway, if it is."

"Then, the nine o'clock."

"I'll be there."

During her second white waking night, she found herself wondering why this man was so accommodating, going out of his way to listen and help.

Was it curiosity about Jonas's fate? About Jonas's ex wife? Or an unaccountable rush of sympathy for an unknown woman weeping into his ear from ninety miles away?

His voice had background in it, education, assurance.

He could be twenty-eight or fifty-five; there was no way of knowing, except that it was a vital kind of voice.

Living in the City of Brotherly Love, his concern might be wholly disinterested and charitable; perhaps he sat on committees to aid widows and orphans.

A memory surfaced, an art director, an old friend, Lou Sims, at Y and R. "I tried to get Gus Welcome, but he's big-bracket and we're not budgeted for him, and in any case he doesn't want to come back here from Philadelphia. Can you believe it? *Philadelphia?* I said for God's sake why, and he said he couldn't think of any good reason for coming to New York and proving that he's better than anyone else in the universe at peddling gas and girdles."

Waking drenched, clutching her pillow for survival, in the middle of a dream about Jonas drowning, the dark water cutting off his anguished cries, her mind whispered:

Maybe *he* did . . . something to Jonas. And feels he has to keep an eye on me, so that I won't . . .

She fell steeply back into nightmare.

Three

Jonas had not turned up in yesterday's Philadelphia *Evening Bulletin*; and now, with North Jersey going by the dirty Amtrak train window, he was not among the morning's fresh accumulation of disasters in the *Inquirer*.

She looked at factory chimneys illegally flagged with purple smoke, soiled meadows streaked with water of an alarming yellow-green, the huge and desolate litter of a landscape wholly industrial. Then she turned to The New York *Times* and read it with great attention, not knowing at all what she was reading.

Five years ago today, the day after their wedding, they had boarded the jet for Paris. She had been startled when Jonas stopped just past the welcoming stewardess after they had climbed the stairs.

"Right here, three-A and four-A."

"But first class?" She had never flown that way before.

"From now on, love," Jonas said, "first class all the way."

Jonas Rath of East Seventy-third Street, a New Yorker born and bred. Blond, sunny, sparkling Jonas, stalking the premises of McKim MacCloud, the large New York advertising agency where they both worked, as if it were his personal domain.

It was her first and last office job; she was now a pleasantly successful freelance commercial artist. A few months after they were married, she said, "I can't just sit here," and Jonas said, "Work, then, work at home—I'm not having you spending your days with the Madison Avenue stallions. It will keep you off the streets, and we can use the money. There's no amount of money we *can't* put to good use."

She had known Jonas as a face and a name for months. He was something of a star at McKim, a writer-producer of television commercials that people talked about. In an orbit well above hers.

And then one wet, late night in spring, Millie and her current man turned up at the White Horse Tavern on Hudson Street, and Jonas and his current girl were there. They joined forces and made a party, and in some strange fashion a fire lit itself between Millie and Jonas.

Four months later they were married. She was twenty-four, he was thirty. Her father came down from the small town in Maine where he ran the newspaper he had bought after several decades on the *Times.*

"Married before, was he?"

"But only for eleven months, years and years ago," Millie said, and then blushed under the gray parental gaze.

"He has charm enough for three," her father said drily. "I assume you know your own mind—" He gave her a check for a thousand dollars, and her mother's pearls, and his questioning blessings, and went gloomily back to Maine.

First class all the way. I just happened to see this in Bergdorf's window, it looks like a Millie dress—hurry, try it on. A hand thrust casually into a pocket, bringing out a little box. It was such a nice day, I wandered into Cartier's and found some diamond earrings for you. . . .

Good-time, hail-fellow Jonas. Champagne-for-breakfast Jonas.

They were having champagne at twelve o'clock on a Sunday a year after they were married. Jonas had fixed his favorite feast and summoned her to it from her bath. The champagne in tall glasses defiantly filled with crushed ice. A bowl of thinly sliced Bermuda onions. Hot crisp buttered toast. Quartered hard-boiled eggs. A half pound of pearly dark gray caviar.

Jonas drank quite a large amount of the champagne. He was philosophizing about happiness.

"I found the secret of happiness long ago," he told his wife. "You know what it is? Love no one. Then you'll never be involved or disappointed. That way, no one can ever get at you, really, you're safe. That's the secret, Millie."

His mood had changed, then, lifted; but she filed away the quiet scald, not wanting to think about it but unable ever to forget it.

It could account for Jonas's total inability, which emerged after that first year, to maintain even a semblance of faithfulness.

"Get him to a psychiatrist," a helpful friend said, finding Millie furiously weeping over her drawing board.

Jonas refused to go to a psychiatrist. "I'm warm and cozy, wrapped up in my little complexes," he said. "I don't want to be stripped bare to a cold world and learn all about being adult and responsible. And God only knows what it would do to my commercials."

Hot and cold. On and off. Reform and then relax. Tears coaxed and teased back into laughter. "What we need is to get away from this rat race for a while, Millie. Let's have a couple of weeks in Tahiti. Let's knock it off. I'll take a leave of absence, we'll spend the summer in Nantucket. Let's buy a boat and spend weekends on the water. You can crew for me, love." They went to Tahiti, spent a summer in Nantucket, bought a boat.

In between, Jonas worked hard and lived hard and made a lot of money. In a way his work and its requirements began to be a sad relief to her. He would be off with a camera crew to San Diego, to New Orleans, to Vail; he would be shooting commercials abroad— Amsterdam, Rome, Cairo—for weeks at a time. The eyes he looked into, the bodies he gently and skillfully cherished, were not visible.

She was working hard herself. She had a big airy studio in their expensive apartment where she could lock out the world, and loss and failure and betrayal. She did fashion illustration at first, of an accomplished and individual kind; then she branched out, freelanced whole campaigns for small agencies not wanting to keep high-priced art talent on their regular staffs. People liked to work with her; she was intelligent and amiable, took care of her assignments fast and well without spattering temperament around.

"I wonder," a friend said, "if your being so terribly good at what you do is bad for Jonas."

Millie didn't think so. Jonas was terribly good at what he did. Or was, up to the last few months or so, before the end of their marriage, when he deliberately seemed to lose interest. Bored with McKim. Bored with his wife. Bored with himself.

She couldn't pretend to a shattered and unbelieving grief when he left her, writing that it wouldn't work, it had never worked, he was bad for her, she deserved better, the biggest favor he could do her was to set her free while she was still young and beautiful, and God bless her, darling.

A bitter draft of rejection to swallow, a middle-of-the-night fog of guilt. (Should she have fought it, gone after him, begged him to come back? No.) An inevitable dwelling on the good things, the happy times, the bright side of Jonas's moon, his warmth and gaiety and funniness, his way of looking upon an hour, a day, as a celebration.

She didn't ask for or want alimony. Her work, by then, was bringing in a reasonable amount. She moved to the pleasant but smaller apartment on West Eleventh Street and was able, within seven or eight months, to think, she was after all an attractive enough girl, people liked her, some people valued her, there were even men who seemed genuinely to want her.

Jonas not helping at all in the healing process, with his long-distance telephone calls and his birthday flowers. A fountain you thought had been turned off, stilled, suddenly leaping and spraying diamonds and rainbows in the sunlight.

She gathered that he couldn't bear not to be liked, even by the woman he had discarded. "It's a cold, cold world out there," Jonas said. "We happy few have to cling together and snuggle in each other's arms."

"North Philadelphia next, North Philadelphia!" The conductor's call came from far away; she had been either half asleep or lost in time, in the past. "Thirtieth Street Station next."

The Philadelphia Zoo on her left, sunlit treetops through the murk of the windows. A plunge into a dark tunnel, then out into the sun again, the Schuylkill boathouses, the Eakins sculls making silver snail tracks on the flat dun-blue river. The Museum of Art, lion-colored, high on its bluff, and the delicate little Grecian temple waterworks below. Strange that the immediate approach to the fourth largest city in the country—ugly and sprawling, as she remembered it from a visit years ago, polluted and fear-haunted, if the newspapers were accurate—should be so fine and fair and green.

Perhaps this same prospect would be on her right, not on her left, as her train pulled out of Philadelphia for New York in a matter of hours. Perhaps there would be a perfectly rational explanation of an imagined catastrophe. An awkward few minutes of explaining to Jonas her mad dash here. And perhaps he was not, and had not been, in this city at all when he called.

The escalator in the station wasn't broken. Dressed as promised in her blue linen suit, and carrying along with her handbag the white canvas suitcase with brown leather corners, she was lifted up on metal stairs to Augustus Welcome.

Her usual incandescence of skin and coloring was heightened by fatigue and a fear of what lay before her. She looked to him unreal as candlelight in the sun, stepping off the grid to the marble floor of the station, bravely braced, her eyes for the moment too large, doe eyes, tilted and vulnerable in a narrow quiet face. She was, in her understated and gentle way, a rather beautiful young woman.

He was standing to the right of the escalator. He threw a long Giacometti shadow across the marble, in the dazzling sunlight. She stopped in front of him.

"Are you—?"

"Yes. And you're—?"

"Yes."

"This is very kind of you. A total stranger—"

He noted that one mysterious small dimple in her left cheek came and went, flickering, as she spoke.

"As I told you, I'm only a few blocks away—"

"But I suppose in any case"—she gave him a doubtful smile—"you wanted to see what manner of madwoman you've been on the phone with."

"Not that, really. I wanted to see what went with your voice. As well as, of course, Jonas—your worrying about him—"

Her face brightened. "Then it's nonsense? He's turned up? You sound as if there's no real need to worry any more—"

As if there's no real need to worry any more.

A man, a stranger, waiting for her. She told herself later that the thunderstruck sense of recognition was illusion. Or exhaustion. A moment passed before he, too, seemed to remember that they were after all people who had not in their lives met until just now.

He took her suitcase from her hand. "I'm sorry, I didn't mean to raise false hopes. No, he hasn't turned up—"

He was a tall, fair man, finely made, large without bulk. He had a forthright Roman nose, a broad patrician brow, long cheek creases that gave his face an amused and skeptical look, and large brilliant gray eyes, deeply set. He was a strong, original statement among the stereotypes that surged around them, the people you see in railroad stations, tired and rumpled, overweight or overdressed, tagged by children. In a tearing hurry or numbly staring, on benches, as if they had always been sitting there, waiting for doomsday.

In a world that seemed to her increasingly androgynous, he came through imperiously if amiably male, like a great green dash of cold refreshing salt water on a sun-hot body.

And there was, perhaps because of this, something immediately reassuring about his presence, as there had been about his voice on the telephone. She supposed that was why she thought the Jonas question had been comfortably answered.

They walked to the east portal of the station, through the tremendous slabs of sun and shadow giant-striding the floor of the great echoing space.

He asked, as they got into the cab, "Am I to buzz Ms. Lester at you, or—?"

"Millie, you're to call me, if you will. Especially as you're going out of your way to take me to the apartment."

"All right, then, if you're Millie, I'm Gus."

She didn't know why she found herself cataloguing every bone in his hand, every hair on his wrist, the exact pattern of his tie, a knitted tartan, blue and brown, a pierce of sun on his eyelashes, and a sudden silver plunge of light, as they turned a corner, into his eyes.

A shyness came over her. She looked with a contrived interest out of her window, very much aware of his thoughtful measuring gaze on her.

Still wondering just how irrational, unstable, given to the pursuit of wild fancies she might be?

The cab went down Kennedy Boulevard, turned right at Nineteenth Street, and in light mid-morning traffic crossed Chestnut and Walnut, went past Rittenhouse Square, its trees and grass butterflied with light and shadow, the Barclay looming gray, turned west, after crossing Locust, into Delancey Street.

He said abruptly, "Look, if you bump into some or any of Jonas's crew during the day, I'd be careful about telling people exactly what brought you here."

She turned her head to him and said in a faraway voice, "Does that mean you think there might be something in what I . . . thought happened?"

"Not necessarily. It's so—" He hesitated and then said carefully, "so damned unlikely. An awful risk for someone. Like televising a private killing. But, the one chance in a hundred, I don't think it would be at all wise to lay your cards on the table."

With a sort of weary dignity, Millie said, "I hadn't planned to play the Ancient Mariner, stopping one of three and boring him into the next century with my tale of woe. . . . I was always sorry for that poor man who had to listen to it all."

"So was I," he said. And added as if in some way to comfort her, "You do go with your voice—"

"What about my voice?"

"It's the prettiest, most—even when describing more or less impossible things. I'm sorry, everything seems a bit unreal this morning. Third house on the right, driver."

The cab stopped and they got out.

He began, she noticed, to speak to her in shorthand, almost from the first.

"An aunt. I'm a comfortably displaced New Yorker. Of course, it's too big for one man, but I like large spaces. I suppose it's one of the last luxuries. Waste space, I mean."

It was a splendid tall brick house, white shuttered, white doored, white fanlighted, in a long agreeable parade of its sister bricks, sunshowered and deeply greened with the movement of the leaves of great sycamore trees.

One man? Then there wasn't, for the moment, a Mrs. Augustus Welcome. Or perhaps she was away somewhere.

They went through a narrow access alley beside the house, its bricks curved spoonlike for drainage, and into a charming large garden. From this, a white-painted iron stairway climbed the towering brick.

He looked down at her face as she hesitated at the foot of the stairs.

Her skin was tinged, now, with blue. Floating specks of light fell into her tea-colored eyes, opened to their very widest like those of a terrified child.

"I'll take a quick look, shall I? See if he's checked in since I left for the station."

To see, for her, if there was anything awful, waiting, at the top of the house in Delancey Street.

Four

It wasn't more than a minute before he ran lightly down the stairs to her.

"Nobody, nothing. Don't look so frightened. Today's payday, and we'll hope for the best. I'm under the impression he's usually somewhat broke, even though—"

Even though he was making pots of money. The situation sounded familiar.

"What are your plans, beyond checking his luggage and things?"

"Look around, and—who knows?—there might be a telephone call or something . . . and place a classified ad, maybe, where are you, Jonas? And generally sniff the air, and then . . . I'm not sure quite what?"

"Will you be staying here?"

"No. If there seems to be any reason for staying overnight, I'll find a hotel."

"Let me know where you'll be, then, in case he surfaces. Here's Homans' number, here's mine. Will you be all right?"

For some reason, she was reminded of lovely safe domestic exchanges—

Well, I'm off. You were short, so I put twenty dollars in your wallet. . . .

I think your blue suit could go to the cleaner's today, and that raincoat is . . . well, wear it once more. Shall we have chicken tonight, or would you rather have lamb chops . . . ?

She came back to a present that wasn't safe and settled at all.

"Yes, Gus, I'll be fine." The first time that she had had that particular syllable, his name, in her mouth. "And thank you for the key, and the lift, and your kindness, if I don't see you again."

Turning to leave her, he looked back over his shoulder in a startled way. Then he smiled and said firmly, "We'll see each other again. Good hunting."

I'll be fine. . . .

All the same, she was badly frightened as she climbed the steps. There could be things up there that wouldn't mean anything to Gus Welcome but might mean horror to her.

The stairway came out on a duckboarded terrace, with a grapevine overhead, under the sycamore branches, making a twinkling green gloom. A cool breezy place this morning. A pair of long rattan chairs, cushioned in faded blue, lounged on either side of a round white-painted table marked with drink circles. The white door, to her left, was washed with green reflections. Gus Welcome had left it ajar.

Just inside the door, on the floor, was an oblong of paper someone must have pushed under it. Torn from a tiny notepad. A quick loose scrawl, "Darling, I rang and banged to wake the dead and no you—please call me, my wandering boy." Signed "A." It would be helpful to find out who A was. Jonas might in turn have found her and be with her now.

She walked into a big living room. It faced north and west; the west window looked out into the green of the grapevines, and more of the green unearthly light leaked into the room and over the dark polished floor.

A wall of books, a handsome black leather sofa, big easy chairs, a cluttered desk with an uncovered electric typewriter on a battered typing table at right angles to it, a Bokhara flaming, rich red and tawny and cream on the floor. Comfortable and pleasant, untidy but reasonably clean, filled to its high ceiling with Jonas. And silent, terribly silent. Except for the murmur of an air conditioner in some room beyond and a faint dripping noise.

A short hall led into a big bedroom. The double bed had been slept in and was unmade. Shed undershorts and socks beside it. On the bedside table was a glass holding an inch of wan straw-colored liquid (Jonas saying, "I'll just have a little scotch lullaby"). A large color television set stood at the foot of the bed. Jonas obsessively

watching, when he was at home, the "Tonight Show" and late
movies—"I'm not keeping you awake, am I, Millie?"—and then falling asleep, and she waking to the gray hum of an empty screen, and
getting up and turning the set off. This memory guided her hand to
the air conditioner. No point in leaving it on.

She opened the door of a large closet. Attractive suits, a lot of
them. A beautiful Spanish suede trenchcoat. Low shelves holding at
least a dozen pairs of well polished shoes. Built-in shirt cabinets
showing stacked delightful colors through their glass fronts. A triple
rack of ties. His luggage was lined up on a high shelf.

All of it was there.

Unless he had added to his collection. Six pieces, brass fittings,
heavy curry-colored canvas, well-used, Italian, expensive.

The bathroom breathed of Jonas. Lime cologne from the West
Indies, tart-sweet. Thick green towels thrust any which way over the
racks. A bit damp in the creases. Lime soap left as Jonas always left
it, to bloat and melt in the waterfilled soap holder by the tub. She
resisted the impulse to take hold of the slippery squelchy cake and
deposit it in the dry soap dish beside the basin, as she had deposited
it so many times.

The medicine cabinet held his usual treasury of pill bottles. Jonas
was a dedicated taker of pills. Shaving brush, damp-dry. Did shaving
brushes ever really dry out, even after forty-eight hours of possibly
not having been used? Razor. Two toothbrushes, one for morning,
one for night. Jonas would never go anywhere without a toothbrush.

The ranks of pills (Millie, darling, won't you join me in an aspirin
—one of these new Yale-blue tranquilizers—some nice antibiot-
ics—?), the smell of lime and the crushed towels and drowning soap
got to her and sent a deep unexpected shock of grief through her.

In this bathroom Jonas was alive, near.

Breathing, and happy, and spared.

Or was it the late Jonas Rath whose apartment she was prowling?

There was a thunderous knock on the front door. Millie stood frozen, for a moment incapable of movement.

A man's voice shouted, "I know you're in there. Work or no work,
friend, laundry's got to be picked up."

She opened the door to a plump little man in a gray coverall. He stared, and then said with a raffish grin, "New tenant? I'm here to pick up and deliver Mr. Rath's laundry. He don't like the bell and sometimes he hides. He don't like to be interrupted at his work—or whatever he's up to"—a frightful wink—"but I always flush him out. We both have our work to do, I tell him."

"I'm afraid there's no laundry ready to go."

"Well, here's the works for this week. Keep well, have a good day, ma'am. Give my regards to the gentleman." He handed her a shirt box and a plastic-wrapped package of sheets and towels.

Where was the linen closet? She found it in the little hall outside the bedroom, put the laundry away, and turned to the kitchen.

How strange. Storing laundry. Answering the door. Walking into the middle of someone else's life. An intimate. A stranger.

In the kitchen, too, Jonas was very much alive. The refrigerator held little food—he had always had a rooted dislike of eating at home before they were married. Eggs, milk, bread, half a dozen cans of beer, two grapefruit, and three cans of jellied consommé—but there, a trademark, was the caviar and champagne for a loving snack for two. Had Jonas been going to bring someone back here—A?—the night before last? Or did he, now, always keep his refrigerator stocked? Just in case of anyone.

There was a used coffee mug on the counter, a half-full drip coffeepot on one of the cold gas burners. At the end of the counter stood Jonas's liquor supply: gin, scotch, vodka, Bourbon, rum. A rack fixed to the wall held red and white wines with expensive labels.

A small radio stood by the bottles. She switched it on. Jonas music, pop.

"If it takes forever, I will wait for you. . . ."

"Close to you, I want to be. . . ."

"I did it my way. . . ."

And then, by an impossible and perfectly ordinary coincidence, Jonas's favorite whistling song, a quiet solemn loveliness, pouring from the radio.

"Shenandoah."

"Across the wide Missouri. . . ."

She must find his personal telephone book, ring all his friends. Is Jonas there? Did you see him yesterday? Or the day before?

Call in a classified ad to the three Philadelphia newspapers. Do that first; it sounded intelligent, active.

On the way to the telephone in the living room, she caught a glimpse of herself in an oval mirror, eyes looking smudged, although she hadn't put on any eye makeup this morning, mouth uncertain, alarmed, the green light wrapping her in a frightening ghostliness—

Discovering the telephone directory in a drawer in the desk, she stopped to study three separate, framed photographs on it. She was very much taken aback to see the picture of herself, black and white, caught by Jonas's Rolleiflex. Leaning against a water-seamed post on a Nantucket pier, two seagulls perched upon it, right above her head, her hair flying in the wind, Jonas saying, "I love the way you look, but for God's sake watch out for those gulls. . . ."

The second photograph was of his sister Olivia, so like him, so unlike him. On some merry late night, he had given her, with a felt-tipped pen, a waxed mustache and a monocle. Olivia. She had to be called, of course. Funny how you forgot that Jonas had a sister. They had never been very close, but Jonas always sent her a large check at Christmas. "Poor old Olivia." She was thirty-seven.

The third, a young girl, with the peculiar current anonymity, long shining blond hair, regular features, sunglasses, jeans, a white shirt. Lounging, hands in pockets, against a white rail fence in a soft countryside. Suggesting Main Line, good school, perfect health, and very little else. She might be "A?"

To the newspapers she dictated a message that sounded to her ears like a meaningless gasp. "Jonas R., please get in touch with Millie immediately, re telephone call early morning June 2, anniversary. Very worried, hurry up." She couldn't give a telephone number, as she had no idea where she would be staying tonight, if she stayed here at all. But no doubt box numbers would be assigned to her, and she would get his answer in New York if, as was very likely, she fled this place, this apartment, this city—

"Rise and shine, Jonas, my boy!"

A hearty cry from just outside the door, a hand on the knob. She hadn't locked it. It was flung wide open and a man strode in and stopped and said, "Oh, good God, sorry. I didn't know he had someone—he's been a bit derelict in his duties again, and I thought I'd just come by and rouse the fine fellow—"

He looked to be in his early forties, a big, slightly blowsy Irishman with startlingly red hair in elf-locks about his balding forehead and cheeks, very pale fair skin flushed with rose like a country boy's, a broad straight nose, a full wide-lipped mouth. He wore a well-cut jersey suit in a Donegal tweed pattern. He generated an air of bounce and affability but Millie saw that his eyes, greenish with pale red lashes, were bright and hard. The eyes moved slowly over her face and body as if he was on some kind of shopping trip.

Not quite a brogue in his voice but a deliberate singsong up-and-down of syllables. Jonas, standing invisibly at her elbow, said, What's he so full of good cheer about? Never trust a professional Irishman, Millie.

"You're Jonas's Millie," he said suddenly, looking from the photograph on the desk back to her face.

"I'm Millie Lester, but not Jonas's any more, as you probably know."

"Ah, more's the pity, more's the pity. I'm James Thomas Ryan, Jim henceforth to you, Jonas's Millie. Creative head and, oh, yes, next president of Homans, nice thriving little local outfit. We're— the new blood, I mean—not Philadelphia, we're New York. Out of the Tait agency. You know Tait—"

Yes, she did. Denture odors and underarms. A special ingredient in an aspirin product that worked three ways better, or was it four? She was silent, letting him continue to display his credentials, and his ego. Who was "we" or was it royal usage?

"Grand town this, though. Just wants to be waked up a bit. We've already lit a few fires—" Then, hospitably, "And what brings you here? I have to tell you that Jonas in his cups feels very badly about you, and the whole thing, and has a soft spot, a very soft spot, for you. . . . He'll have been glad to see you, young woman."

She found this offensive but kept her face quiet.

"I don't like to be tactless," Ryan said, with a kindly, we-know-what-it's-all-about grin, "but do you think he could be gotten out of bed? It's"—he glanced at his watch—"pushing twelve. Hell of a fellow, Jonas, old friend of mine, we worked together at Tait. It was

I who hauled him from Chicago and set him up on his velvet cushions as a consultant. Couldn't get him any other way, the lazy devil. This afternoon, though, we need him, we really need him. But there it is, he was always a night man and a devoted morning sleeper—"

"Was."

She stared and he stared back at her. In the silence, she heard the faint dripping sound from the kitchen.

Why not, "He's always been a night man . . . ?"

Was.

"Jonas isn't here," she said. "I've come down from New York on a matter of family business, and I'm just as anxious as you are to get in touch with him."

Ryan sighed. "Bedded down somewhere else, then—oh, sorry, didn't mean to—poor girl, ninety miles for nothing, maybe. I won't disturb you any longer. If he does wander by, tell him to call me immediately, will you? You'll be here all day?"

"Perhaps. And yes, I'll have him call you if he wanders by."

"There's a dear girl." He lifted a hand in a friendly salute and left.

Had he been really, as he said, trying to rouse Jonas from a late morning sleep? Or had he come around to see if everything was quiet, settled, finished, at Jonas's apartment—no policemen poking about.

Watch out. Here's how and where the fantasies would begin to take her, suspicion in a shadow, danger in an intonation.

For instance, she had had a sharp strong feeling of danger, close, while the two of them, she and Ryan, listened to the tap dripping into the silence.

Of course that one small word didn't mean anything except that Jim Ryan was a sloppy talker, mildly mishandled the English language.

But . . .

Was.

Five

The police. She should have called them right away, when she got here. The hunting of missing persons on one's own, however, took training; she really should be doing seven or eight things at once, not brooding about Ryan's misuse of tenses.

Switched from extension to extension at police headquarters, she was finally allowed to identify and explain herself. A pause while records were sought. "Oh, yes, you're the woman who called from New York six-two-seventy-five, 1:41 A.M., reported hearing possible gunfire over the telephone. Man named Rath. He hasn't shown up at any of the hospitals. I'll switch you to Missing Persons if you want—"

"Can't I see someone there? I do think there may be"—find the correct, sinister word—"a homicide involved—"

"Well, without a body, ma'am—you know, we happen to be pretty busy around here. But okay, I can give you a few minutes at three-thirty. Detective Sergeant Valiante."

She went through Jonas's red leather book and made seventeen fruitless calls. The eighteenth call was to Olivia in New York. No answer.

Restlessly, she went out to the terrace for momentary escape from Jonas's scent, his voice, his presence.

A head, at her knee level, thrust through the tangle of grapevine and ivy that made a living, rustling wall opposite the door.

A voice said officiously, "Are you looking for someone?"

Millie started, then realized there must be an adjoining terrace on a lower level, at the back of a house on the next street over, Cypress.

The face was of a woman probably in early middle age, with a disappointed mouth sending two lines to her jawbone, intent pale blue eyes and gray hair in a Dutch doll cut. She radiated a hostile curiosity. Her voice was high and nasal with a slight affected drawl.

"Yes. I'm looking for Jonas Rath."

The blue eyes regarded the slightly open door into Jonas's apartment.

"I *must* say you go about it informally."

It wouldn't do to have her nervously summoning the police.

She identified herself, adding, "I used to be married to Jonas." A near and listening, perhaps eavesdropping, ear, might turn out to be helpful. Her manner friendly and open, she said, "I had to look him up and couldn't reach him by phone, so I thought I'd come on by."

"Oh, yes, of course, he's talked to me about you and your picture's in there—" An acute study of Millie's face and her hair, hazel-colored and luminous, cut in thick loose petals which dipped and glowingly rearranged themselves whenever she moved her head. "Except your hair is shorter now." The hostility had vanished; the face in the vines fairly twitched with curiosity.

An arm penetrated the green barrier, holding a glass. "Will you join me? I'm Dora Maunder, and I've just started my vacation so I'm allowing myself a pre-lunch drink."

"Yes, thank you, I will." She was tired, and thirsty, and sensed in Jonas's neighbor a rich source of information.

"One of Jonas's—or I guess really Gus Welcome's—railings is missing here, but there isn't quite room to squeeze through. Go down your stairs and I'll run down to my door."

Dora Maunder talked her up three flights of stairs in the Cypress Street house.

"Heavens, you came to the right place. I'm good friends with Jonas. Formalities: I worked at Homans for eighteen years, wound up as executive secretary to Mr. Homans, and then that pair, Ryan and his creature, turned up from Tait in New York, and thought I didn't fit their new image—no long hair or legs or anything—and I was fired. Mr. Homans is semi-retired, and I thought naturally I'd work for Ryan. Not so. I don't think Gus Welcome would have let them do it, but he was away shooting commercials in California when the ax fell. In any case, he's sold his shares back to Homans and doesn't sit on the board any more. This happened just a week or so ago, you can imagine I was slain. But I picked up another job right away, luckily, with Capstan Insurance. . . ."

There was pain and bitterness under the lightly chattering voice. Millie sympathized; she had watched in New York advertising agencies the fear as the age of forty overtook people, the male changing of hair styling and coloring, and wardrobe, the female dieting and the desperate attempt at the makeup un-madeup gloss and gleam of the very young. She thought it all sad, and cruel. . . . Go take your talent, and experience, and all you've learned and developed to a high fine polish, and jump into the East River with it. . . .

". . . But the dear souls are kindly paying me for two weeks' vacation—which I'm going to spend comfortably right here, so nice to turn over and go to sleep again when the slaves are rushing to work— and gave me five hundred dollars as a down payment on my room in the old folks' home. Here's my little aerie in the sky."

Her little aerie had a yellow awning, yellow director's chairs, and a glass table on which reposed an ice bucket, a bottle of vodka, and a saucer of quartered limes.

"On the rocks? With or without tonic?"

"With, thank you."

"You do look a bit exhausted and as if you could use that," Dora said. And then, a little resentfully, "When I'm tired, I look tired. You look like a lily in need of watering," studying her with a naked objectivity which Millie found trying. The pale blue eyes pricing her linen suit, deciding whether her sandals were Italian, and was that her own hair color?

Millie did a little summing up of her own. More an elderly girl than a mature woman; unrealized, lonely, and now flatly rejected. She obviously, from the way her voice handled his name, adored Jonas. And would have received, from him, something in return— Jonas had a soft, responsive heart—a drink, an endearment, a careless hug.

Physically, she was short and small, in a white shirt and white pants that suggested, at the hips, a dumpiness not far away. Draining her glass, she refilled it and gave her full attention to Millie's business.

"Now, about Jonas. Does this visit of yours have anything to do with the police coming the night before last?"

Millie considered, looking into her drink. There was a marked, personal interest here.

"I was talking to him, that night, late, and there were sounds over the phone that could have meant some kind of . . . accident. I haven't been able to reach him since, so I thought I'd come have a look."

Dora's eyes sparkled. She was openly fascinated.

"What sort of sounds?"

"A shot, I think, wild as it may be. . . . I called the police, but Jonas wasn't at the apartment. I have no idea, as a matter of fact, whether he was even in Philadelphia when he called. . . ."

"Oh, he must have been in Philadelphia. I saw him running down his stairs after nine that night, in that divine lilac linen shirt of his"— she giggled—"and trousers, of course. He certainly wasn't carrying any luggage. I called to him to come up and have a drink, but he said he had to meet some people."

In a delayed reaction, she said, "A shot—!"

"Was he all right? Healthy? Well?"

"He was *gorgeous*," Dora said. There was a sudden sharp line between her eyebrows. "You're not thinking that he—that the sounds —that he could have shot himself? While he was talking to you?"

The idea had hovered, as a thin unthinkable possibility, at the back of her mind. Jonas's strong sense of drama, and his recklessness. And the basic despair which must always have lain under his, *I found the secret of happiness. Love no one.* . . .

"Never!" Dora said violently. "He has too much to live for." In her frightened anger, she turned hostile again.

At least she wasn't using the past tense. Between the lines, she was saying, Kill himself for you? Are you crazy?

". . . He has a fabulous job at Homans, consultant, two days a week, comes and goes as he pleases, he's making a ton of money. Of course he drinks and parties a lot—why not? Attractive, to say the least, and unattached. But he always looks the picture of good health—"

"Well, good," Millie said. Dora would simply not allow Jonas to be dead, and this was momentarily cheering. "But you can imagine how—frightening it is, particularly as I don't know how or where to find him."

"You've come to the right person," Dora said, placated. "You must rely on me absolutely. I'll do whatever I can to help. It's fortunate I'm on vacation. We'll track him down in no time. Put yourself in the hands of Detective Maunder."

Millie suspected that the Jonas mystery was a godsend in what had been going to be an inexpensive, dull vacation taken at home. Especially as Dora seemed so sure it would have a happy outcome.

"Of course," Dora said, with a curious mixture of lasciviousness and jealousy, "if he's shacked up somewhere and doesn't *want* to be found, that presents difficulties. You said he wasn't there when the police came. I was out doing Wanamaker's and Strawbridge's yesterday, all day, looking for shoes. My feet are—well, never mind. And he wasn't there last evening, but he often isn't. Could be that he couldn't quite make it home, was somewhere he didn't want to drive his car from, I must say he's good about not driving when he's high. . . ."

"He does have a car then?"

"Yes, one of those Japanese ones—I forget the name, dark blue. He leaves it on the street, any old block. People do that here. Sometimes paying all the parking tickets is cheaper than garaging the car, and *he* never pays them anyway. I'll go looking for his car later, see if it's around."

She sipped her drink. There were bright excited circles of pink on her cheeks. "To get back to *cherchez la femme*. His latest is that stupid rich girl, Main Line, all sorts of money and of course she's more or less engaged to Aldington."

Her eyes narrowed in sudden speculation.

"I wonder. I wonder if Aldington could have done anything to Jonas."

Six

Aldington, as described by Dora, was the host of a local television show, "Good Morning with Aldington."

"I assume he has a first name, but he never uses it. The few people he'll deign to talk to call him Aldy. Tall, young-old, if you know what I mean, a snob, arrogant, insolent. Makes no attempt to hide it, and do you know the fool women around this town and out in the suburbs drink it up and beg for more?"

She was herself, Dora said, no radical, in fact politics bored her; but he was so conservative in his views he made Broad Street bankers seem positively Red. He had been born of an old, wealthy Philadelphia family whose wealth had vanished; was in every way a product of money. Had an exquisite carriage house on Delancey Street where he gave small elegant parties. "I've never been to one, even though I've known him, to say hello to, for years. He's in and out of Homans all the time. One of our—their—big clients is one of his sponsors. He does the commercials himself for them, live, so of course he has to work closely with our"—she blushed and pushed an impatient hand at her gray bangs—"with the copywriters."

His show, running from nine until ten weekdays on KGY-TV, was well sponsored, both by local and national advertisers. "I suppose he makes good money at it, but with people like that it's real money that counts, the kind you don't have to go out and soil your hands to earn."

His putative fiancée, Amanda Graves, of the Paoli and Nantucket and St. Croix Graveses, would have that kind of money.

"But then Jonas reared his handsome head. . . ."

She didn't suppose it would last long, but you never could tell. She thought it must be a bitter blow to Aldington. "Anyone laying even a *finger* on what he considers his property—" Serve him right, but still, he had a nasty and violent temper, she'd seen it in action, very hot and very cold at the same time.

"Your descriptive powers are admirable," a man's voice said above their heads, behind the green leafy screen. A cool, haughty, rather high voice. "—If, one might reasonably add, prejudiced."

Dora, her face red, leaped to her feet and spilled her drink. She moved her mouth convulsively, but was speechless.

Millie, after the first stunned seconds, got up from her yellow chair.

"Are you Mr. Aldington, and if so, what are you doing on Jonas's terrace?" Ridiculous, maddening, to address grape leaves and ivy, swaying softly in the breeze.

"Jonas was to appear on the show next week. We had an appointment to discuss the approach this morning." The tone calm, precise, with a suggestion of, If that's any of your business.

"Please wait there a moment." Millie saw Dora out of the corner of her eye, refilling her drink with a trembling hand. She went quickly down Dora's steps and up Jonas's, and came face to face with the tall, thin, slightly stooped man. The stoop suggested a seigneurial bending from the heights, to see what all those people down there beneath one were like.

He had pale icy eyes in a long narrow face pink-tan from the sun. His clothes looked deliberately old, good, English. He held a pipe in one hand, a glossy chestnut leather attaché case in the other. He was motionless, very much at home as he gazed back at Millie. Thirty-five, maybe.

She wondered how long he had been there and how much he had heard. About himself. About Jonas.

"For someone so carefully got up as a gentleman, you don't quite know your lines," she said.

He smiled without warmth. "Eavesdropping, you mean? But you don't know how fascinating it is to hear a seminar being conducted on oneself. . . . Alas, they're right when they say you'll hear no good. Are you going to tell me now who you are and where Jonas is?" He glanced at his watch. "My time is pretty carefully parceled out."

"I was his wife. I have no idea where Jonas is. I'd like to know that myself."

He looked at her ringless finger. "Oh. One of those." Effortlessly offensive. "Well, I've rung and waited and rung again, and there's no answer. I suppose there's nothing to do but take my leave."

"I didn't hear the bell ringing." She pressed it and the sound was clear and shrill. She remembered that she had left the door unlocked.

Beginning to descend the steps, he turned his head and said, "No doubt the sound of the bell was drowned by the hearty tinkling of your ice cubes."

She opened the door and went into the shadowy living room and stood still, sensing his recent presence there. This was soon confirmed. The photograph of the blond girl leaning on the rail fence no longer stood on the desk. But that, she thought, was probably by the way, an instinctive scooping up in passing. How long had she been with Dora while he made free of the apartment? And how long had he listened on the terrace? She had been gone fifteen, twenty minutes at most.

"That was a lie, about coming to see Jonas about appearing on his show," Dora said from the doorway. "It would be a game of, you come to my office at the studio, you have the time and I haven't. Besides, they hate each other, so a casual visit would be absurd."

"Have you any idea what he could have wanted in here?" The note signed A was in her pocket, and he could hardly have known about that anyway.

Dora flopped onto the leather sofa. "Dear God, my knees are still shaking. Now, let's think. Some sign that Amanda's been here? A dropped lipstick or something like that? Incriminating letters? A forgotten girdle?" She laughed. "No, those girls don't wear girdles." And sourly, she dragged at the waistline under her shirt, making an adjustment.

Millie was thinking that Jonas's apartment was a popular gathering place this morning.

Dora all attention, watching, listening, explaining.

Ryan coming cheerily by to rouse his lounging consultant.

Aldington on some browse of his own.

Even Gus Welcome, so kind. Going out of his way, examining the apartment before he would let her go up his stairs.

"Does Jonas always live—surrounded like this?" she asked Dora. "Do people keep coming in from right, left, and center stage?"

"More or less," Dora said. "He knows everybody and he likes company."

She caught Millie's tired polite glance and got up off the sofa. "I'm in your way—I'll be off. I'll take a stroll around, later, and see if I can spot his car." Her air of being not wanted hung uncomfortably over both of them.

"I'd appreciate it—the car, I mean—and there are some calls I have to make."

She tried Olivia again, remembering belatedly that of course she wouldn't have been at home. She had been running for a year or so a boutique in New York on MacDougal Street, Olivia's Village.

"Millie who?" Olivia, answering, asked absent-mindedly. "Oh, yes, *Millie*. How are you?"

"Have you seen or heard from Jonas in the last few days? I'm in Philadelphia looking for him and he's not here."

"I haven't seen him for months." A sudden quickening of interest. "Is there anything the matter?"

She was his sister and ought to be told. Millie told her.

Olivia was silent for a moment and then said devastatingly, "I'd better come down there. After all, I'm his sole heir, I expect. You don't plan to put in any sort of claim in case anything *has* happened to him?"

"For God's sake, Olivia!"

"Well, anyway, I'll be there tomorrow at the latest. There must be all sorts of things to be seen to. I wonder how much he's insured for. He used to carry fifty thousand, and I'm told he's been making vast sums. . . . And it would be nicer for you," careful change of voice, a softening, "if you had company, looking around for him. I'm a bit strapped for cash—I imagine I can stay at his place, seeing he's not there?"

It was a naive idea that people of the same blood were supposed, if not actually to like each other, to extend decencies to each other. There had, however, been Jonas's generous if last-minute Christmas checks to his sister. Maybe his casual bounty made things worse.

"If his rent is paid, now that we're on financial matters, his landlord probably won't object to your staying here," Millie said in a voice that was, for her, harsh.

"Oh, and Millie, I'd appreciate it if you wouldn't touch his mail. I'll go through it, if he isn't there when—" What was she afraid of? That his former wife would find a check and forge his name and cash it?

His insurance. His mail.

His laundry freshly put away, and the lime smell in the bathroom.

Funny, Jonas, you don't look dead.

A crackle of paper in her pocket reminded her of Amanda Graves. She found the number in Jonas's red leather book. A butlerlike voice informed her that Miss Graves was away from home.

No, sorry, madam, he had no idea where she could be reached and when she would return. She had left, taking her car, several days before, and was there any message? Yes, I will have her call you, madam, when she is at home again.

". . . of course, if he's shacked up somewhere and doesn't want to be found, that presents difficulties. . . ."

As punctuation, a passing truck in the street below backfired, an ear-blasting noise that rattled the panes in the windows.

Seven

Philadelphia police headquarters was housed in a bizarre figure-8-shaped building on Race Street, officially called the Police Administration Building. Millie, having signed in at the main desk and received instructions as to where to find Detective Sergeant Valiante, got into a round elevator crowded with laughing, chatting, backslapping policemen, black and white.

She had the faint sense of undiscovered wrongdoing that many an innocent feels when completely surrounded by police.

A duty officer on the fourth floor took her name, muttered it into the telephone, and in a minute a man in a gray suit came out and took her into Detective Valiante's office.

She took the seat he indicated, across from his desk and facing the uncomfortable slatted dazzle of venetian blinds.

He was thin, dark, and tired-looking. His red-rimmed eyes suggested that he had been forced onto day duty after night duty. The yellowish color of his skin hinted at a poor digestion and so did the sharp odor of peppermint in the tiny office. He looked blankly at Millie as though some strange bird had flown in at his window to occupy his other chair.

Still feeling she was being had up for something, she explained her marital status, gave him her professional, and maiden, name and her New York address and telephone number. "I can't give you an address here yet. I haven't had time to look for a hotel room."

He laughed without amusement. "I hope you like sleeping on park benches, Mrs.—Miss—there are four conventions in town." He gave a deliberate long glance at his watch and tapped a folder on his desk.

"I've read the report on this matter. Thought you heard your ex shot, did you? I have to say first and foremost it's pretty hard to pinpoint particular sounds in this big rackety town."

His tiredness, and his communion with his watch, made her feel apologetic; a silly woman on a wild mission.

"Not after back alimony, I assume?" A faint grin. "In Pennsylvania, you're wasting your time. If there was a child, now—"

"No, I don't get alimony."

"How long have you been divorced?"

"Two years."

"You're awfully—anxious about this fellow. What's the connection?"

Impossible to explain the business of her delayed answer to his call, the guilt, the feeling that she had inadvertently sprung some fatal trap on Jonas. And then, he breathed and he laughed and he was a living creature. . . .

"I thought it was the least I could do, to see if anything had really happened to a man I was married to for three years."

She saw in his cold dark eyes his disapproval of divorce. She would be lumped, in his mind, with all divorcées. Hard demanding straying women; or conversely, not warm and tolerant and forgiving with their men. Breaking up homes when they should have been staying put, with Tide and Maytag and pasta, taking care of husband and kids.

His glance, catching hers, bore this out. "It's maybe a question of property, money? You want it proved he's dead so that the way'll be cleared for you to collect?"

"No question whatever. And I don't want it proved he's dead. I'd much rather it was proved he's alive."

"Well. As you know, people disappear all the time. For reasons of their own, reasons that don't concern us. If he was a dope addict, or in any way abnormal—say a child molester—had any kind of record, of course we'd be interested. As it is—"

"As it is?"

"The noises you heard or thought you heard. Look at it yourself. One, either it was a combination of natural noises, and he just forgot he was talking to you; it was late, maybe he'd had a few. Or, two, he was fooling around with a loaded gun—people do, you know—and it went off by accident and maybe wounded him, maybe did nothing but go off and make a big noise. Or, three, someone with him might have let off a gun accidentally and might have panicked and not reported it. He might be under someone else's care, maybe a wounded foot or hand or something. As he isn't at his own place, he'd have to have been with someone in their home or apartment when whatever happened happened. We'd have heard about a bar shooting. A friend, a buddy, or, who knows, just someone he got talking to in a bar might have— Would he strike up an acquaintance in a bar?"

"If he was drinking, I suppose—yes, he might."

"You have no idea, Mrs.—Miss—how crazy people can be. If I could write a book—anyway, my advice to you is, maybe put a notice in the classified, wait and see what turns up. His friends and business associates may have information. We'll do a little checking. If it all turns out to be zero, go home and forget it. Tell yourself he wanted out, one way or another."

His alternatives were all equally, confusingly possible, even rational.

"I suppose if explanation four, or five—I've rather lost count— came along, that he *was* really killed, you'd do something about it?"

He flushed angrily. He snapped, "We have a ninety to ninety-five percent figure of solved murders in this department. But to have a murder, you have to have a body, not just a funny noise and a guy you can't find right off the bat when you come charging down from New York." The glance at his watch, again. "We've had four honest-to-God murders, complete with bodies, in Philadelphia in the last day and a half."

She got up to leave. "Just one more thing, Sergeant Valiante. What do you think about a private detective . . . ?"

He shrugged. "We have a saying that a private detective never solved a crime, and you seem hell-bent on a crime. Anyway, can you afford upwards of a hundred dollars a day and expenses?"

"I don't want to, no."

"Check with me if you decide to go that route. The good boys, our retired men, are mostly in security, you know, big business stuff.

You don't get the better class of men chasing down divorce dirt—oh, pardon."

She thanked him, made a note of his extension number, and went down in the elevator and signed herself out at the desk. She had to tally, beside her name, the time. Three fifty-three. The police had given twenty-three minutes to what might have been the violent termination of thirty-five years.

Feeling whipped and demoralized, and like someone in the process of becoming a public nuisance, she went down the broad shallow steps into the white heat and glare of the afternoon.

In the cab going south, along a grim stained street of potholed cobblestones and broken pavements in a rundown business district, she wondered what good, if any, she had accomplished. Probably a sop to her conscience, nothing more. (Well, I did go to the police. . . .)

The first hard certainty about what had happened to Jonas was now as elusive to grasp as a handful of mist. It could have been this. It could have been that. Or the other thing.

If you're alive, and well, and happy, and amusing yourself, Jonas, I'll have your head.

I'll have your head. But with part of it shot away—

The driver saw her face in the mirror and said, "You all right, lady? I thought—"

"Thank you, I'm fine. . . . It's hot." She had given him the Delancey Street address. Her bag to be collected at the apartment. A hotel reservation to be made, in spite of the four conventions. Eat something, sooner or later; she had forgotten about lunch.

There might be answers to her ad in tomorrow morning's mail. A lot of things, clarifying helpful things, might happen tomorrow. Give it to the end of the day or perhaps to the middle of the following day, and then go back to New York.

Forget it. Tell yourself, yes, Sergeant Valiante, you're right; he wanted out, one way or another.

Halfway up the white stairway, she heard the telephone ringing. Fumbling with an unfamiliar key in a temperamental lock, she prayed it to stay ringing. It did, suggesting someone stubborn, determined, at the other end.

Her hello was breathless.

"Is Jonas back?" A man's voice, without color.

"Not yet. Who—?"

"Shattner here. Amos Shattner. At Homans." And then, rudely, "Are you the wife?"

Tired of explaining herself, and not liking the sound of Amos Shattner, she said, "If you have a message for him, I'll take it."

"I do. I thought I'd just warn him, as a friend, to get his ass in here no later than tomorrow."

Odd that a single sentence could convey jealousy, an attempt at brutality, and at the same time a sort of cringing. She cast back over Dora's gossip. This was Ryan's copy teammate from Tait.

"—and while I have you on the line," Shattner said, "will you tell your pal Dora Maunder to mind her own fucking business? She called Mrs. Shattner to find out if she had heard anything from Jonas yesterday, roused her out of her nap. She's just got over the flu, she was pretty damned mad. Dora rambled on about you—if you're the wife—worrying about him, and said she was calling everybody she could think of. She's a troublemaker. She'd better watch out."

Millie looked at the instrument in her hand and replaced it on the receiver.

It started immediately to ring, sounding furious.

What had she been going to do? Have something to eat—

Her eyes hazed. Jonas's grandfather clock, inherited from his Aunt Elizabeth and standing facing her to the right of the door, seemed to lean alarmingly forward. As if it intended to fall and crush her.

Hardly knowing what she was doing, she kicked off her sandals and half placed herself, half collapsed, on Jonas's black leather sofa.

Eight

At a little after six, Gus Welcome went speedily up the white-painted back stairway and wondered at his haste.

He had been worrying about her, vaguely, on and off all day. Face to face with her clear-eyed intelligence, he found her theory about Jonas much harder to dismiss and explain away.

Late that morning, ". . . he's off somewhere amusing himself, or *them*selves. . . . I stopped by in the hopes of finding him and stumbled on little Mrs. Jonas. She's looking for him, too. . . ." Ryan's hearty voice, a few feet from his office door, talking probably to Shattner, in the next office.

"Inaccurate on two counts," Gus said, without turning his head from his work at the drawing board. "She's not little, she comes up to my shoulder, and she's not married to him anymore."

Ryan beamed in at him from the door.

"You an old friend of the lady's, Gus? Hell of a good-looking girl in her quiet way. After you've finished with her, it's my turn."

His grin faded under the gray, brilliant, unsmiling gaze. "Bless me, I keep forgetting I'm in a nest of Quakers."

Gus did not trouble to explain that he had only met her this morning. Which now seemed to him odd; she was already familiar to him, known from a long way back. He disliked Ryan's voice relishing her, Ryan's large confident feet striding her personal territory.

"I'm a bit busy at the moment," he said. "Why don't you go next door and play darts with Shattner?"

For just the portion of a second, Ryan's amiability fell off him like a costume dropped to the floor, and a naked animosity showed in his pale green eyes, tightened his broad mouth.

Then he grinned again, walked over, clapped Gus on the shoulder, looked down at the casually dashed off and stunningly good full-page newspaper layout on his pad, said, "Terrific, I mean terrific. I'll leave you to your own devices, fella. . . . Lunch?"

"Sorry. Can't." They had had lunch, once, in the five months since Ryan and Shattner had arrived from New York.

To smooth for himself the untroubled curtness of the refusal, Ryan laughed and said, "Your local girl, I suppose . . . ? We all know you're above and beyond business lunches like the rest of us poor commercial slaves . . ." talking himself jauntily into the hall.

He did have lunch with Virginia. In the middle of a martini, she said, "You're not here, Gus—are you making layouts in your head? Come back to me."

He had been, then, where he was right now, following Millie Lester. Up hill and down dale. Looking for Jonas.

In her haste to answer the telephone, she had left the key in the lock and the door several inches open. He gave a slight householder's shake of his head at this. Didn't she know that even green and pleasant streets in Philadelphia were regularly robbed, with rape here and there, murder just around the corner . . . ?

His finger almost touching the bell, he hesitated. Perhaps she was trying to catch up on her sleep. She had looked to be approaching exhaustion, at the station.

But in any case the door couldn't be left this way. He opened it and went into the living room and stood looking down at her.

Profoundly asleep. Vulnerable white throat; one arm and one long leg dangling to the floor. Defenses gone.

He thought how easy it would be to kill her, asking for it as she was, coming here with her eccentric story, and in a fumbling kind of innocence trying to clear up the question of what, if anything, had happened to Jonas.

"Millie." He said it carefully and quietly so as not to frighten her.

She stirred and half waked and he saw it on her face: there was something difficult and strange and sad to absorb her, but for a few seconds she wasn't sure what it was.

Then she blinked and sat up abruptly and turned a candlelit and reassuring pink. "My God"—her eyes going from his face to the grandfather clock—"two hours! And I have to—"

She yawned distractedly and pushed back tumbled petals of hair, revealing a high rounded forehead.

She felt lost, nowhere. To have this man come and find her asleep in a crumple of blue linen when there were things to be seen to, things to be thought about—

"In case you haven't gotten around to it, I have a hotel room for you," he said. "We keep a suite at the Bellevue for visiting firemen, and it's nice and empty. Living room, kitchen, bedroom, and bath. Will that suit you?"

If it had been anyone else, she might have had reason to be wary. Find her a room, and then you'll know where she is, alone, and how to get at her in case—

But right now, tired as she was, she accepted with surprised gratitude.

"You're being terribly nice. I can't think of any particular way to thank you—"

"You need food and drink," he said, casually, companionably. "You can thank me by coming downstairs and having it with me. I'd take you out to dinner but you're probably not up to it. And if there's anything at all you want to know about Homans, and Jonas at Homans, I can fill you in thoroughly."

It was that last statement that made her say yes. Otherwise, the burden of imposing on a stranger would have been too heavy. But Jonas was the reason why she was here, and he would know things about his work and the people he worked with that she couldn't possibly find out by herself.

In a subterranean way, she had wandered to the conclusion that whatever had happened had something, in some way, to do with Homans, Inc.

Dining at Gus Welcome's house emerged as a positive duty. "Give me fifteen minutes to shower and change, and then I'll ring your front doorbell."

"No need to go out." He crossed the room and used a key in a door to the right of the linen closet. "Just come down the inside stairs. Leave the door open so you can hear the phone. When did you last eat? I'll cook you something while you change."

A year ago. . . . "About seven something this morning." One cup of coffee; she hadn't been able to swallow food.

She took a fast shower and got into the only change of clothes she had brought with her, dove gray pants and tunic in a soft silky jersey that touched her body loosely and lightly.

Feeling curiously shy—most of her business, after all, was done with men, art directors, and she was usually very much at home among them—she opened the door to a wide descending flight of stairs with a walnut banister like satin under her hand. Her thin-strapped gray sandals, on bare feet, were almost soundless on the steps.

Amplitude surrounded her, the releasing feeling of large generous spaces in a dwelling built for grace and peace and comfort. Fascinating glimpses, through open doors, a yellow bedroom, a blue and white one, then a broad landing, its window full of blowing shifting green. Something that looked like a study with late sun slanting across a creamy old Kirman. The final flight down, long and curved, to the wide handsome hall. It, and the rooms off it to her left and right, must have ceilings fourteen feet high.

How quiet it was. Where was he, and where was the kitchen? In a house of this size, there wouldn't be revealing odors to guide the nose. She looked into a living room, tall, white, a perfect wallow of space. Comfortable and pleasant, used and inhabited—the *Times* left tumbled over a chair arm, a forgotten coffee cup on a windowsill; rather bare, with a fine golden-yellow marble fireplace, a silver blaze of mirror over it, deep chairs, books, pictures, old Persian scatter rugs on the dark shining floor, ten-foot windows gazing on sycamores and brick. The right room, somehow, for Gus Welcome.

Behind her, he said, making her jump a little, "Do you mind the kitchen? Everything's hot. Come on, Millie, I'll show you the way."

He took her hand and led her through the dining room on the other side of the hall, formal and festive at the same time, through a vast butler's pantry and into a big square kitchen. Surely he didn't have the care of all these glistening surfaces and shining objects?

There was a table at the window overlooking the garden. He had broiled steaks for them, and made a salad, and heated crusty airy French bread. Millie fell on her food without ceremony, as a suddenly urgent physical need. He watched her with pleasure.

"Don't talk with your mouth full, Millie," she said. "Delicious—marvelous—" She sipped wine and felt herself coming alive, able to think, able to ask questions. Over coffee, she said, "Now tell me. About Jonas's job. And Ryan, Mr. Good Cheer. And Aldington. And someone named Shattner who uses obscenities over the phone to a woman he's never met—"

"He did? To you?"

"Yes. I live in thickets of four-letter words and normally don't mind, but somehow from him they were a fist in the face—"

"I can now allow the patient a decent drink, and we'll get away from the pots and pans and go settle down, first. Scotch, I think, very nourishing."

He carried their drinks into the living room and they sat down on a brown velvet loveseat facing its mate at right angles to the hearth.

Obediently, he began:

"Jonas's job. He's a consultant, whatever that is. He works portions of two days a week for forty-five thousand dollars a year, on contract. He seems to be a sort of window dressing for Ryan. Comes in magnificently turned out to client meetings—the golden boy, the expert, loaded with awards and medals—and drops names and cities, Procter and Gamble, Campbell Soups, General Motors, Exxon, Chicago, Cannes, L.A.—of course he calls it L.A." He hesitated. "I also have a feeling that Jonas has something on one or the other of the unholy pair, and got his job here on the leverage. I may be wrong, and perhaps it isn't fair to throw that in."

Millie snatched at it eagerly. "Jonas knows everything about everybody, always has. It's a sort of hobby of his, finding out. He can offer you the most scandalous information on what you thought were perfectly respectable people—but then you know him. . . ." A little guiltily, she added, "He's fascinated with human nature, much more so than I am—that's the other, good, relishing side of his being a gossip and a sort of snoop—"

She looked down at her hands and said in a small remote voice, "It's getting hard to stick to the present tense. Should I begin saying, He *was* . . . ?"

Gus was silent, watching her. He finished his drink, eyed hers, still half full, and went out to the kitchen to get himself another one, bringing back the bottle and an ice bucket with him.

She hadn't moved. Her head was still bent. He went over to her, took her hand, drew her to her feet, and put his arms around her and held her, very gently and kindly.

She moved, without thinking, a wanting inch closer against him, his comfort and warmth in a darkness that was seeping in on her.

"Good." The voice so close, vibrating. "You're moving in under my eaves."

She raised her face to him and he kissed her mouth quickly and lightly. Her senses recorded, indelibly, his lips, warm and moist-dry, muscular and delicate on hers.

Almost absentmindedly, she said, ". . . I was more or less thinking about being married in July, or August. I thought June was a bad month. . . ."

For a moment she thought something had happened to his eyes, after a sudden blink. Then, "*Are* you." He said it in an interested tolerant way, studying the face under his. "Anyone I know?"

What an ass I am, she thought, suddenly wretched. A man feels sorry for you, gives you a spontaneous hug to cheer you, and you shove your private life, your marriage plans, at him. Unhand me, sir. . . .

Completely mistaking his intentions.

Half-drowned in embarrassment, she moved away from him and picked up her drink and rattled the ice cubes, giving them all her attention.

"Mike Garland. Garland Studios, television—but I suppose you might—"

"Yes, I know him, I've worked with him." Calm, neutral voice. "Very good man. Professionally speaking, I mean—I've had no occasion to analyze his character." Nice of him to notice nothing, talk as if she hadn't delivered herself of a maidenly Victorian flutter at his hearth.

Not touching her, he gestured to her to sit down and went and sat down on the loveseat across from her.

"Where were we? Before we celebrated your engagement? Oh, yes, Ryan—"

Talk. Talk intelligently. After all, that was what this evening with Gus Welcome was all about.

"I saw him this morning, and I think I got part of his picture. Very jolly, and overflowing with good nature and . . . hard."

"Also lusting after power, which he's about to get. Alex Homans is ready to pull out, he'll be president in a month or so. Partly a matter of money—he and Shattner have begged and borrowed and sunk everything and more than they've got into Homans stock, including Brunhild's money. . . ."

"Brunhild?"

"Mrs. Shattner. I believe her name is Alma. Anyway, Ryan. Married, two sons, a dedicated wanderer after women, winker, rump-pincher—I don't know whether it's for show or whether he does sleep variously around. All this while keeping you relentlessly up to date on his sons' progress in football and the Little League and his wife Goosey's—yes, you heard it right, Goosey, her name is Gertrude —cooking and den mothering."

"For an art director," Millie said, "you're very articulate. I can see it all, I've met other Ryans."

"If you don't mind, let me be who I am and not a member of a tribe." He said it mildly, but she felt herself flushing. Yes, how offensive of her, to inform him he could speak the English language in such a way as to make himself understood.

He laughed a little and said, "One way or another, and without intending to, I seem to have you on the griddle. It's pretty when you blush, but it can't be all that comfortable from the inside out. I wasn't scolding—and you're an artist yourself, Millie, you're in no position to throw stones. For a number of reasons, you need another drink, I think."

She told him that Aldington, too, had stopped by at the apartment. She didn't add the suspicion that he had been searching for something; it sounded not quite real or sane enough to put into words now. That poor Lester woman . . . she's had it. Delusions of romance, of searches and persecutions. . . .

"Strange man, cold," she said. "I got the feeling, standing near him, that someone had opened the freezer compartment of the refrigerator—"

Gus said thoughtfully, "Jonas was about to recommend that his show be dropped, the thirteen-week option comes up next Tuesday. But I hardly think he'd reach for a gun because he was losing a sponsor, even though it's a big one, a key one, Guardian Petroleum—"

Dora: Aldington has a nasty violent temper . . . very hot and very cold at the same time.

Continuing her mental dialogue out loud, she said, ". . . and Jonas was borrowing his girl, if Dora Maunder is right . . . Amanda Something. . . ."

"Borrowing other people's girls is disgraceful," he said lazily, in a voice that was no longer neutral but warm and amused.

"You mentioned"—she had no idea now, what her position was with him, whether she was being charmingly laughed at or not—"something about the unholy pair. Is Shattner the other half of it?"

"Yes. I suppose turning worms are possibly dangerous. Ryan uses him and then pets and rewards him, a vice-presidency, plenty of money, a wall knocked down to make an office almost as big as his. He's Ryan's sounding board and prompter, and for all I know all Ryan's ideas could be his. He bows deeply to people he thinks are important and bullies the secretaries, worries about extended coffee breaks and makeup sessions in the ladies' room. Rich wife, German —he is too—who takes over the pushing around at home when Ryan's off duty. He seems for some reason to be crazy about her. Or maybe he just likes the whip."

"I'm told that he and Jonas hate each other."

"I don't know about hate, on Jonas's side. He treats him with open contempt—"

The telephone rang as if from somewhere high in the treetops.

Gus said, "I'll get it—three flights—" and went like an antelope up his stairs.

Coming down, he said, "Dora. She says she can't find Jonas's car.

She has walked sixteen blocks. She has something else to communicate to you that she's keeping to herself. I gave her your extension at the Bellevue."

He had brought down her bag with him. It seemed a good time to exit, and there were a lot of things she wanted to, and didn't want to, think about, alone.

"Thank you very much for what there isn't any way I can thank you for." Being taken in, cared for, fed, warmed, held, hoteled, supplied with trenchant information. And affectionately kissed.

"I imagine I can find a taxi—"

"Evenings are bad, in this part of town. Call a Yellow Cab and wait a week or so, and then it will come. I'll walk you down, Millie, it's not far."

It was after nine, deep purple late June twilight.

"Walnut, I think, more people and more lights," Gus said. He looked twice over his shoulder as they crossed Eighteenth Street. "Don't be alarmed, but there seems to be a man following us, or you. While I was on the phone, upstairs, I saw him standing in the doorway across the street, deep in a newspaper with not enough light to read it by. Wait here a moment."

He parked her in the brilliant light streaming from Nan Duskin's windows and went rapidly back to the south side of Walnut Street. Millie saw a small shadowy figure turn and run scuttlingly but fast, away from him.

Gus rejoined her in a few minutes. "He went down a dark alley beside the Warwick with the accuracy of a rat. I don't somehow like the idea of a knife between my shoulder blades. Let's get you to the hotel fast. There may be nothing in it—he could be just going our way, or interested in your handbag when I leave you. Or he might be just a normal neighborhood crook. Did you see him well enough to spot him if you saw him again, trailing you up the street?"

"Yes, I think so—his way of walking and running, small, harmless-looking, shabby—"

Under the canopy of the Bellevue, they were surrounded by what must have been one of the four conventions in town. "Welcome, Square Dancers of America," a banner on a car at the curb said. Gray-haired women in glasses with great starched crinoline skirts and flat dancing slippers; gray men, thin or pear-shaped or both, gallantly arm in arm with them.

Giving her her room number, he said, "I'd take you to the desk, but I'm going to stand here for a few minutes and see if our friend shows up."

Millie looked up at him, gay for a moment. "Don't get mixed up in any square dances, Gus. Not your style."

"I had an idea on the way down," he said. "There's a job I have that I think would be just right for you—if you're not too expensive, that is. Will you come and see me at Homans tomorrow morning, or whenever you wake up? That way, you can examine the rogues' gallery firsthand. And that way, I can keep an eye on you."

He kept his eyes on her as, turning, smiling, she went up the steps.

Then he watched the milling, flying skirts, calico and gingham, listened to the flat Midwestern voices. Turning his head, he thought he saw the small shadowy man, but before he could make certain, the man, part of a batch of bodies, disappeared downward into the Walnut Street subway station.

Nine

Dora Maunder was, as she had been all day, in a state of unaccustomed and delicious agitation, helped on by holiday vodkas.

Forced by finances to vacation at home, she had thought, fine, plenty of time to sleep, and then she'd maybe take a good long look at every painting in the Barnes Foundation, perhaps visit Du Pont's Longwood Gardens, see the old, great houses in Fairmount Park she always felt guilty about having missed, go to Wilmington and really go through Winterthur, spend hours in the Museum of Art. It would be, yes honestly, fun.

Even if she had the money, a vacation alone lacked a certain something. She might be able to squeeze in a day or so at the shore with her sister Ellen and her brother-in-law Joe, but Ellen had said in her bright crisp way:

"Don't plan too hard on it, Dora. The children may be having friends to stay. Of course, we'd love to have you, if there's an empty bed."

She had no one in her life now, no one of her own.

Her mother, of whom she had had the care in what she thought of as the crucial years, when a girl could get herself married, had died three years before.

For some time, Dora had had an arrangement with a man from a type house she had met at Homans. He spent two nights a week at her apartment while presumed by his wife to be in Wilmington, where he had a number of clients.

But Dora tired of the secrecy, the on-and-offness of it, the loneliness, and the deep jealousy that she felt for his wife, and began to press him to get a divorce.

There were scenes, quarrels, a series of attacks of hysterics on her part, and the man she thought of as her lover retreated in April to the safe domesticity of his home in Blue Bell.

Then today, along came what she had already begun to call the Jonas Affair.

That attractive ex wife, so ready to listen, so interested in what she had to say.

And now heavenly Gus Welcome seemed to be in a way involved. She had seen him from her deck, racing up to Jonas's door, watched him go in the door and then—no one at all had come out.

How odd. But of course there was an inside stairway. And people live by different rules now, Dora thought enviously. They might just have said hello, good evening, nice to meet you, and fallen onto Jonas's bed. She considered, in mid-drink, the two fine bodies exchanging enjoyments.

Her blood stirred. Drama and excitement—and very possibly sex—instead of the empty days, the now unappealing schedule of visits to museums and gardens.

Rumblings of the great world that lay outside her neat, quiet apartment. Mystery . . .

Intriguingly terrifying thoughts of doom, disaster, death. Life in full blazing colors, instead of black and white.

The pulse of her two free weeks throbbed and quickened.

Of course she didn't want anything to have happened to Jonas, she reassured herself. His very presence next door provided vicarious daily glamour.

Sometimes he'd ask her to his parties. "Come early, Dora darling, and make some of those hot cheese puffs of yours."

She had dropped hints, as she did every year, about her approaching birthday. Ellen and Joe forgot, everybody at the office forgot, but Jonas didn't forget.

There was a party on his terrace just for the two of them, champagne and caviar, and a beautifully wrapped present. She fingered it now, a slender bracelet of golden fleur-de-lis.

And Jonas's best present of all, a strong arm, a sweet kiss. "Don't give up the ship, Dora. You know the saying, about marriage, There's a lid for every pot? And you're a very nice well-heated attractive little pot. . . ."

Unfortunate things did *not* happen to people like Jonas, living his life with a relish and recklessness that made the very air of his apartment heady to breathe.

How nice it would be if she, Dora, could clear up the whole question. Track him down. It was just a matter of patiently exploring one possibility after another.

Yes, it would be very nice. In the end, make a kind of airy joke about it.

Guess who found Jonas for you?

Dora Maunder, who wasn't good enough, young enough, glossy enough for Homans after working there eighteen years.

You have to hand it to Dora. There's never been anyone like her for downright efficiency. . . .

Her phone rang. It was her sister Ellen.

"Hi, Dora. I had to bring Jessica into town to the dentist and we're at the apartment. I thought I might kill two birds with one stone and go to dinner with Evelyn—you remember Evelyn, and her new husband. She's been at me for weeks. Will you baby-sit? I ought to be back around eleven or not much later."

Baby-sit? Dora frowned at the invisible Ellen, who was trying to drag her back into everyday drab when shining vistas were opening to her.

"Well, I don't know, I'm pretty occupied. I'm helping a friend from New York with a problem, rather a big thing—"

Ellen's voice warmed a little, coaxing. "I think, by the way, the weekend after this might be a good time for you to drop down to the shore. Bobby's going to stay with some little friend in Connecticut."

"That would be fun, if I'm not all tied up on my other thing," Dora said coolly.

"—and you know Jessica's no trouble. And she's so fond of you. She said on the way up, 'Will I see Aunt Do?' Remember how she christened you Aunt Do when she was a tiny one?"

Dora, knowing she was being conned but needing what Ellen was saying to her about her niece, said reluctantly that, all right, she'd be over as soon as she got dressed.

Ellen's apartment was in a brownstone-fronted house on Spruce Street. Ellen, who was a version of Dora, but dimpled, dark-haired, and eight years younger, kissed her on the cheek and said, "I've unsheeted your favorite chair and there's a little vodka, I hope it will do. Kiss Aunt Do, Jessica."

Jessica was five years old. Her hug and kiss were warming and thoroughly meant.

"She's had her dinner. Bath and bed in half an hour. I bought a nice frozen beef pie for you. Have fun."

Have fun, indeed. Dora eyed the vodka bottle. One halfway decent drink, if that. And trust Ellen not to have any tonic. She would have to make do with ice and a little water.

She turned on the television set for Jessica. Ellen liked Jessica to be creative in her before-bed playtime, look at her books or dabble with her paints or crayons, but these cultural accessories were at the shore. Jessica sat on the floor and stared at an old Western.

Dora, in the slipper chair by the window, looked out into the purple evening. She tried to recapture her sense of excitement, of involvement. Of not just being Dora, Aunt Do, convenient to call on for baby-sitting and other family tasks, because everyone knew Aunt Dora wouldn't be doing anything any particular evening.

Well, start them. Start with A, for Aldington.

He was the very first person who had come into her mind when Millie, on her deck, talked about something awful that might have happened to Jonas.

She knew from close friends at Homans that Jonas was loud and clear about his intentions to recommend to Guardian Petroleum that they cancel out on "Good Morning with Aldington." The option would be coming up early next week. What if—

It was time to put Jessica to bed. Dora tucked her in and kissed her. These simplicities made her idea seem a little, well, crazy. But the real world *was* crazy sometimes.

What if Aldington had stashed Jonas away somewhere so he wouldn't be around to raise objections when the option came up for renewal? Ryan, she was told, was of two minds about it, and Aldington could go to work on him without interference. A kind of businesslike kidnapping—

She put the frozen beef pie into the oven, wished in vain for another drink, ate the pie, washed up. Then she ran up the stairs to ask Mrs. Pullen in 2A (a dedicated snoop anyway) to keep an eye and ear out while she went to the corner for milk.

After a look at the deeply sleeping Jessica, she took a small flashlight from the drawer of the hall desk, and quietly left the apartment.

Aldington's house was only two blocks away, one over, one down. She didn't exactly frame in her mind what she was looking for. The helpless waving of a handkerchief at a high window, or bars newly set in front of the panes— It was just that it wouldn't hurt to take a quick stroll.

Patiently explore one possibility after another.

Dora had never been in the house, but she had seen a camera tour through it on "Good Morning with Aldington," seen several programs filmed in his garden.

It was a remodeled carriage house, its bricks painted black, its windows shuttered in the palest blue and balconied in black iron lace, with white tubs of pale blue pansies flanking its white door.

Yes, there was someone there. A light in a window upstairs. Other than that, the housefront had no message but style.

The garden was at the rear of the house. Might as well take a look. She went around into Latimer Street, feeling nervous. A woman alone in the gathering dark—but it wouldn't take a minute—

There was, as she remembered, a house being rebuilt next door to Aldington's walled garden. She found, with the help of her flashlight, an untidy heap of concrete blocks. She stacked three, climbed up, and peered at the back of the house, and the garden. A young moon helped.

Another light, downstairs, behind heavy curtains. Had he just not switched off a lamp upstairs, or were there two people in the house?

The garden was long and narrow. There were no flowers at all. Dark arrowy cypresses, alternating with slender marble columns topped with classical marble busts, stood facing each other against the side walls.

A round pool lay like a great dully shining coin, flanked by marble benches. She had read somewhere that you could murder someone by holding them face down in the shallowest of water, but then of course Jonas wasn't supposed to have been drowned, but shot.

She cautiously switched on her flashlight, half-covered its glow with her fingers, and directed it downward. At the inside of the rear garden wall, a bed perhaps three feet across revealed itself, the earth freshly turned over. Following it along, she found it ran the whole length of the wall, eighteen feet or so.

What was Aldington preparing to have planted here, she wondered. Deadly nightshade?

She almost laughed aloud at the thought. Really, investigating other people's premises—in a worthy cause, of course—was rather fun.

Eighteen feet. Not one, but three graves' worth. How simple. The earth spaded and ready. She shivered. No, not fun.

"Stand still or I'll shoot," an icy male voice said from the shadow of a cypress tree three feet away.

Dora shrieked and dropped her flashlight onto the soil below. His own pencil of light played on her white, openmouthed face. She could just distinguish Aldington's features, and his tall threatening figure.

"It's only me, Dora Maunder. Do be careful, Mr. Aldington, do put your gun away." Horrible black thing in his hand.

"And just what are you doing, peering into my garden? I've a good mind to have you arrested for trespassing, or reconnaissance for future burglary. . . ." Along with his outrage his voice conveyed an amused contempt.

"The cat," Dora cried. "I'm so terribly sorry, but I'm baby-sitting for my sister, she lives more or less around the corner on Spruce Street. It's a valuable cat, an Abyssinian, and it got out and ran down the street. I followed it and I thought I saw it jump onto your wall and down."

In a desperate squawk, she called, "Here, Nero, Nero!"

"You've got your geography mixed up, as well as, I suspect, your errand here. Please remove yourself immediately. As a baby-sitter, you strike me as a deplorable failure."

Hating him, Dora said stiffly, "If you wouldn't mind picking up my sister's flashlight—"

After all, an innocent neighborly thing about a lost cat—you'd expect a little sympathy, a little help in looking around for it. Already, she half believed in the cat.

"Thank you for being so kind, Mr. Aldington," she said with what sarcasm she could muster.

He had the last laugh, a high, rasping laugh.

"Good luck," he said, "with your corpse-hunting."

Ten

". . . Yes, corpse-hunting, those were his actual words," Dora said, sounding out of breath. "Of course, he'd have heard you on the terrace, about the shot, and your being worried about him. It doesn't have to mean anything, anything at all—"

Millie had just stretched out a grateful body on an enormous double bed, one of two, in a large room formally window-swagged and curtained and slipcovered in quiet brown and white.

Dora heard the sigh of fatigue and said resentfully, "I hope I'm not boring you, it's just that I thought you'd be somewhat interested. I was at a—a party and our host's cat escaped, and we all went out to look for him. I thought I saw him jump into Aldington's garden. Well, the cat wasn't there, but there was a great long trough of freshly turned earth, like, you know, like a—"

"Like a grave," Millie said to Dora's faltering.

"He spotted me and came out. He had a *gun* in his hand—he was furious, or maybe terrified, I don't know which. . . ."

"I don't quite see what I can do about it," Millie said wearily. "You can't just wander into somebody's garden with a spade and say, 'Mind if I do some digging here?' But thank you anyway, Dora. I wish you'd think now of taking care of yourself and enjoying your vacation. . . ."

She was beginning to feel Dora as a responsibility she was not at all anxious to take on. "I don't want you involving yourself in possible danger. Don't—don't just walk into something blind. It could be awfully bad."

"Thanks, but I'm a tough one," Dora said, cheerful again. "Speaking of tough, earlier today I saw Jonas's bottled water—he can't stand the stuff from the tap, we call it Schuylkill Punch—just sitting in the sun at the bottom of the steps, getting boiling hot. I somehow managed to carry the case up all those stairs and put it in the shade to keep cool. . . ."

Bottled drinking water for a man who might lie deep in a garden trench. The thought of such a burial was so unacceptable, so grotesque, that Millie put it from her in outrage.

That's what gardens were for, digging up the moist soil, planting things—shrubs, flowers—in your reassuring little patch of domestic earth. Part of normal everyday life. Sunny and healing.

Firmly holding in her mental vision a quiet place of sparkling shadow, like Gus's garden, roses nodding, white petunias curling and foaming . . . perhaps a butterfly or two . . . yellow, or blue . . . she watched the butterflies . . . flickering . . . hovering . . .

She tumbled off a high cliff of exhaustion into sleep.

She woke, gasping, trying to scream, to the worst terror of her life.

A hand on her shoulder, in the impenetrable blackness. A sound of breathing—somebody's face, bent close.

She could neither move, nor think, nor manage any sound in her paralysis. Her heart felt as if it was going to burst.

Later, she wondered how long the hand was there, on her shoulder. It could have been half a second. Or a full minute.

The hand tightened slowly. After a timeless interval, a man's voice, a few inches away, said, "What kind of a game do you think you're playing?"

Her throat produced a sound: a tiny half-sobbing gulp. The hand was removed. There was fumbling, an ashtray hit the rug, and then the bedside lamp was switched on.

The light showed the man to her, standing upright now. No knife, no gun that she could see, the large heavy hands at his sides.

The light showed her to the man, white, then suddenly green and sweating, her eyes immense: a rabbit frozenly waiting for execution.

He was staring at her, breathing hard, panting—or was that she, panting?

"Uh—sorry," the man said. As if, in an elevator, he had stepped on her toe. "I was to meet someone here in the suite. . . . The living room lights were on and I saw an evening newspaper, but the bedroom door was closed and I thought . . . I didn't know how you'd gotten in, I mean the person I . . . then I thought, maybe tipped a bellboy or something, wants to surprise me, so I decided, play along, don't turn on the lights. . . ."

He looked to be about forty, medium height, but broad bulky chest, high strong shoulders. His hair was crimpy-curly, dyed a brown-blond color. He had a nose too small for his face and eyes like blue lamps, curiously without expression. His mouth was small and petulant.

Millie came back very slowly, it seemed to her, from a zone totally frozen and bound in silence.

"Who are you?" she said, not recognizing her own voice.

"I hardly see that that matters, seeing that you're the wrong—"

Middle-education kind of voice—familiar in some way. Expensive cream-colored suit a little too wide in the lapel. Orange and white striped shirt, orange tie—self-conscious swaggering way of dressing that didn't quite come off.

"As you very nearly gave me a heart attack, and there still may be a question of my calling the police—" With a bravery she hadn't imagined in herself, she shot out a hand to the telephone and began to lift it—"I'd like to know."

"For Christ's sake put that phone down." The harshness, the naked hostility, identified him for her.

"You're Shattner. Homans—"

His eyes turned sly. "Maybe I am. And who are you, and what the hell are you doing sleeping in the agency suite?"

Hardly a time for an answering hostility on her part, alone in the night with a man with large strong dangling hands.

"I'm Millicent Lester. Gus Welcome kindly lent me this room."

She had a feeling he had known who she was, at least when the light went on, and that he was now going into some kind of act.

"Hell of a nerve Welcome has, dossing down just anyone here at the drop of a hat. You shook me up so I hardly knew what I was saying. Actually, I was working late and came here to catch up on some notes. I didn't want to drive out to Strafford at this hour and wake up the whole house. Thought I'd snatch some sleep and be able to get into the office early, sevenish—work stacked up to here—"

She stared at him unblinkingly, hand still on the phone.

"—it'll be your word against mine, about why I wanted the suite. No witnesses, so don't try to pull anything—"

Under the bullying, she sensed a shrinking cowardice. A whine had crept into his voice.

"Shall I call the desk, or will you leave immediately?"

He hesitated, looking at her with hatred, a look she had rarely encountered and found coldly shocking.

Vicariously directed at Jonas? Or was it because some careful disguise had been ripped off, and he had been caught out in his amorous midnight fumblings?

Or because he had wanted her throat, and somewhere lost his courage—?

"Of course I'm leaving. I'll just have to find another room, late as it is—damn everybody and everything." He turned and picked up an attaché case he had left on a marble table by the bedroom door. Without so much as a glance over his shoulder, he went stiffly, high-shouldered, out the door. Waiting, she heard the almost-slam of the door beyond the living room, leading into the corridor.

She lay back, tense, studying the ceiling, and wondered if it would ever be safe to go to sleep.

There was a commotion at the front door, a spirited attack on the brass knocker and doorbell. Gus, exploded awake, looked at his watch. It was after one o'clock. He pulled on a robe and ran down the stairs, preparing for disaster. Jonas's body found, the police—

The woman standing at the top of the white marble steps said, "Sorry if I woke you. I caught the eleven o'clock from New York and came straight here. Have they found him? I mean, has he turned up?"

"Jonas?" He looked at her in a bemused way. A startling family resemblance, but what worked for him didn't work as well for her, the square white teeth and big handsome nose and large head, and the height. She wore an elaborate white-blond wig that had nothing whatever to do with her style and her features, and a severe striped seersucker pants suit.

Her voice didn't go with the rest of her: it was low and womanly, and a little vague.

"I'm Olivia, his sister, Rath. I talked to Millie and she didn't think you'd mind if I stayed in his apartment while I help look for him and take care of his affairs and mail and so on. He's so careless, and someone might make off with things—my father's gold cufflinks are very valuable, and there are the black opal ones, and I know he has a habit of keeping cash around, lots of it. And there's Aunt Elizabeth's grandfather's clock—heaven knows what that's worth—"

This might very well go on all night, the listing of Jonas's possessions.

He suppressed a yawn and said, "No, no sign of Jonas yet. If you don't mind, I'll just give you an extra key. There's a light switch to the left, at the bottom of the stairs in back, just leave it on—"

"Thank you," efficiently, "I'll find my way up. Do go back to bed, Mr.—"

"Welcome."

"Well, thank you . . ."

"No, that's my name. Augustus Welcome."

"I see. In any case, good night. Thank you for the key. You've nothing to worry about, I don't smoke in bed or anything like that."

She turned and vanished around a corner of the house.

He had just gotten into bed again when the telephone rang. Shattner, voice shaking with some kind of indignation.

"Welcome?"

"Who else?" Gus asked irritably.

"Look here, what the hell's the idea of making free with our suite at the Bellevue? It's strictly understood that it's for client use and in emergencies for agency personnel of a certain bracket. I went in there after working late, to catch a little sleep, and found that woman in bed. I tell you, it was damned embarrassing, and I was put to the trouble of going down to the desk again and—"

Gus gave him a curt three-word directive and hung up.

Shattner, stumbling in on a peacefully sleeping Millie. Charming surprise for her. He remembered how she looked, asleep, helpless white throat, a sweetness about the mouth and the gently rounded brow.

He lay awake for a while, worrying. One way or another, she was asking out loud for trouble.

Sleep did come, after two nights when there had been little of it and two very long, strange days. She drowned in it and woke after nine to a climateless timeless room, the light on because she had been afraid to go to sleep in the dark, the heavy curtains obliterating day, the air neither cool nor warm but neutrally conditioned. Must banish this small, immediate unreality to be able to deal with the larger one—

She pulled a cord and the day came in, dark, pouring rain, but real. People down below, on Broad Street, going about their business, going to work, doing real things. A snarl of traffic, buses, taxis, trucks, sluicing water. She hadn't thought to bring a raincoat or an umbrella but such things could be bought.

She showered, put on the silky gray pants suit again. It would probably be chilly, but the blue linen suit was hopeless; remember to have it pressed. She wished, with an interview with Gus Welcome ahead of her, that she had a closetful of clothes here. Frivolous, seeing why she was in Philadelphia, but perhaps the beseiged mind found comfort and stability in the minute-to-minute daily questions: What will I eat for breakfast? What will I wear? Is there a shop in the Bellevue where I can buy an umbrella? There must be.

She almost missed it, but not quite—"Good Morning with Aldington." She switched on the color television set and got the last seven minutes of it.

Aldington's interview setup seemed to Millie typical of the man. Two Barcelona chairs at right angles to each other, a low round marble table with Aldington's pipe rack placed on it. He fondled various pipes while he talked, tamped tobacco, but didn't smoke. No one but a tall man like Aldington could sit with any comfort or grace in a Barcelona chair. Mies Van der Rohe himself, when he was asked why he had made the chair so deep, had said he supposed that it was because he was a large man.

Today's guest was a woman whose play *The Kingdom* had opened three nights before at the Forrest. Apparently, it had to do with the presidency and the White House, and all the members of the cast were characterized and costumed as animals. Millie had read, on the train, a disastrous review of it.

The crushed tired-eyed playwright was forced to an awkward, almost apologetic position on the edge of her chair.

Aldington, close up on camera, looking much more pink and tan than she remembered him, hair glossily side-parted and Englishly brushed, directing a thin creamy smile at her.

"One gathers your best audience is doting grandmothers bringing in their grandchildren . . . to see all those darling animals talking like real people in the Administration. I wish you many grandmothers, Miss Fagan—and, since you see the world in animal terms, exactly what sort of animal would you characterize *yourself* as?"

Her flush was painfully visible. Aldington held up a hand. "Oh, sorry, we're out of time. Let's hear something interesting from Guardian Petroleum." A pious filmed commercial about the energy crisis and what the folks at Guardian were doing about it. Visually stunning, verbally overloud, annoying, and unconvincing. She felt in it the unlikely clashing mixture of Gus Welcome and Ryan. And perhaps Shattner.

She was about to turn away when Aldington reappeared, alone on the set.

"Speaking of animals leads us to dogs," he said. "I don't normally do this, and pray don't ask me to do it for you out there, but a good friend has asked me for emergency help. He's lost a dog named Jonas in the area west of Rittenhouse Square, in or around Delancey Street. He is, I'm afraid, a mixed breed, rather light in coloring, and wears a license, is in fact quite licentious." A thin laugh through his nose. "If you see such an animal, answering to the name Jonas, please call the station switchboard."

Millie was unutterably shocked.

"A dog named Jonas."

Why? Idle malice? No, not malice—contemptuous cruelty. Just for fun, for kicks? Perhaps Ryan had asked him to help find his consultant, and this was Aldington's way of doing it. Or it might be directed to the ears of Amanda Graves, wherever she was, whomever she was with.

Okay, Jonas, I'm on your side from now on. No matter what you've done, or gotten yourself into, I'm on your side.

Reminded of Amanda, she called the Graves house again and was informed that Miss Graves had not yet returned home. No, madam, I have no number for her.

Given courage, by Aldington's insolence, to do something tactless and necessary, she called KGY-TV and asked to be put through to him. He turned out to be as difficult to reach as the head of the CIA. Voice after voice: And who is this, and what is your call in reference to? They were very much afraid he was not available at the moment. Probably he got, along with devoted telephoned praise and adulation, furious expletives, shouts, threats.

Finally, she told a fourth voice, "It's about Amanda Graves. It's terribly important."

He came on immediately. "Yes, who are you, and what about Miss Graves?"

"We met yesterday. Millicent Lester. Can you tell me where I can reach her?"

"Why on earth," Aldington asked, "would *you* want to reach *her?*"

"A mutual friend," Millie said smoothly and coldly, knowing he would know it was a lie, knowing he would know why she wanted to find out where Amanda was, "told me to look her up."

"I wasn't aware that Amanda had mutual friends with anyone in trade," Aldington said insultingly and ridiculously. "But, you can inform your friend that she's . . . on a yacht, off the coast of Massachusetts, the yacht's intentions being, among other things, the Elizabeth Islands . . . and, yes, Monhegan. She neglected to inform me whose yacht it is, so unfortunately I can't give you a ship-to-shore number."

"You're very inventive, Mr. Aldington," she said. "I could hear you making that up as you went on. Naturally, *you'd* have to seem to know where she is."

"Perhaps I am inventive. And you, Ms. Lester, are very impudent. And, I would say, under the circumstances, rather daring."

Eleven

The receptionist-switchboard girl took her name and looked sympathetically at the great stain of water up one side and across the front of the brand new geranium red raincape she had bought in a shop at the Bellevue.

Millie said ruefully, "While I was waiting for a cab—it took quite a long while—"

"It's a sport in this town," the amply breasted, silver-pink blond girl said cheerfully, "to drive real fast close to the curb when the streets are overflowing and drown the pedestrians, or at the very least ruin their clothes." She shoved in a plug and murmured into her mouthpiece, "Hey, your worship, you have company. Ms. Lester. Just got here, all soaked."

Millie had called earlier, from the hotel. No fiddling about with secretaries, and who is this calling, please, but Gus's voice, right away.

"Sorry, I slept late. When shall I—?"

"As soon as you can make it. I gather you had a visitor last night."

She was silent for a moment, puzzled; it seemed out of character for Shattner to tell tales on himself. But yes, he would want to get in first with his story of a virtuous night alone, catching up on his notes and his sleep after working late.

"Yes. Have you ever been so terrified that for a little while you don't . . . exist?"

"Not yet," Gus said. "Get a cab now, right now, and you might keep an eye out to see if there's anyone following you."

He came out to the reception room to get her, reached out his hand to her, and guided her down a long orange-carpeted passageway with rows of offices lined up on the window wall of the building. Outside each, a secretary typing, or filing, or drinking coffee, or giggling on the telephone. Then around a corner, and left again, into a big comfortable well-fitted office, warm and bright against the dark day and the rain dashing itself against the panes.

"Normally I don't present myself for a job wet and dirty," Millie said, gesturing at the splash.

"Here, take that off—"

"No, I'm still cold. . . ." She shivered a little. She couldn't bring herself to tell him about Aldington's reference, on the air, to Jonas, couldn't somehow put it into words. It hadn't been in any way a good morning.

"He did follow me, I think, that gray man. In a sea of umbrellas, it's hard to be sure. And the back window of the cab when I got one was smeared and all streaked with rain, but I think he was in the taxi behind me. It didn't stop here, at your building, but slowed and then went on as I got out."

"No wonder you're feeling a chill," Gus said slowly, considering her, considering the man following her. He couldn't be a very skillful operator if he could be spotted so easily. "Sit down and I'll get us some coffee first and get you warm."

She looked from the big deep couch to the cupped, padded pedestal chair beside his drawing board and went over and sat in the chair. "It's homier here by the board."

When he came back with the coffee, he asked, "What actually happened last night that frightened you so badly?"

"I woke in the pitch dark to find a man's hand on my shoulder and someone's face a few inches from mine."

"My God, Millie, I thought you'd just heard his key in the lock and gone to the door or something—why all this, in the dark?"

"He muttered at first about thinking I was someone else, someone he was to meet, playing games with him. Before he recovered and retracted it and went on to his next tired-businessman story."

"*Shattner?* But I thought—" He looked straight in front of him and then gave a quick, dismissing shake of his head. He said, as if returning from something interesting but not immediately important:

"Your ex sister-in-law turned up after one last night demanding entrance."

"I'm sorry," Millie said automatically, then remembered that she had no responsibility for Olivia's occasionally eccentric behavior. "We both had our night visitors."

"I called her before I left the house and of course"—the "of course" now seemed a natural phrase—"nothing. She was going through his mail."

His telephone rang twice and was dealt with, during his Olivia information. A girl with a layout in her hand came to the door, cried, "Help, Gus!" looked in, hesitated, said, "Oh, sorry," and went away. A stout man came in with a batch of four-color proofs that he placed on a large table and said, "Have to see Gillins. I'll be back in five minutes, Gus."

Gus was obviously a very busy man; she felt uncomfortable, having to have the coffee to warm away her chills, the man following her, an ex in-law and a problem of her own cluttering up his office, his house, his day.

"Now, if you'll let me see what it is you want me to do," she said, alert, businesslike.

The telephone rang again. He picked it up and said, "Oh . . . hi . . ." two rather soft syllables, obviously not addressed to a man, and half turned from her. She had a dread of sitting, looking as if she wasn't there, while people took personal calls in business offices. She had always thought the listening and watching and waiting during such calls a rude procedure. Quickly, she got up with her paper cup of coffee and went out into the hall, out of hearing.

From the office next door to Gus's, she heard voices that she recognized. It must be a large office, because she could see in on a slant, through the open door, chairs beside a round table, thick blue carpeting, part of a corkboard wall, but not the speakers.

". . . hey, fella, what about this: a kid saying to his mother, 'Mommy, what's a guardian angel?' That way, develop the thought, you know, translate it into modern industrial terms, we could make Guardian look pretty damned saintly. . . ." Ryan.

"For God's sake, Jim." Shattner, sour. "You can't mess around with religion. You'd get the Catholics in a stew. What about that other idea you were playing around with, the Night Brigade, Guardian at work while you are sleeping, a guardian never sleeps."

"I thought about it," gloomily. "I really gave it a lot of thought, and bless us all, you're too modest. I think it was *your* idea. But what bothers me, and right me, fella, if I'm wrong, is that the great unwashed out there will think, Sure they're working while I sleep, hauling in billions of dollars. It takes day *and* night to stuff away all that money."

"Millie." Gus's voice from his doorway. "Come back in. . . . That's the first smile I've seen out of you this morning."

"Advertising taking place, next door," she said. "They haven't quite hit on the right thing yet, but no doubt they'll get there. Now, if you'll just show me your job—"

There was a layout for a full-page color newspaper ad on his board. Dominating it, dashed down quickly and loosely but with style and authority, a girl in a long calico dress and a calico kerchief sitting in a maple rocker holding a calico cat. A big crisply lettered headline: "Old-fashioned goodness for pernickety cats. . . . Along comes Calico Catfood." At the bottom of the page: "A new product of Friendship Foods."

"Finished drawing on this," Gus said. "Has to be endearing, if you know what I mean. Your girls look that way anyway, but no corn, contemporary, very clean but not tight, lots of color. If it's sold across the board—"

His phone rang again. He picked it up impatiently, listened a moment, and then handed the receiver to her. "For you. Long distance, Rome."

He got up and left the room.

Mike Garland, loving, murmuring, "God, I miss you—what on earth are you doing in Philadelphia? I thought your answering service was around the bend—"

No time, now, for Jonas and all the ramifications, in somebody else's office, on somebody else's telephone. And anyway, he might feel he ought to be there, and he had a tremendous amount of work to get through, his time budgeted down to the last minute.

"Doing a job for Homans, Mike." The "darling" which usually

followed didn't come to her tongue. Private lives were for private places.

"I had to hear your voice. Someone's screaming at me. I must go— call you later. Homans? I know Gus Welcome there, look him up. *All right, I'm coming, for Christ's sake.* Take care, love, that's after all my body you're in charge of. Don't get into any Amtrak derailments on the way back."

A full minute passed after she had hung up. Then Gus came back, resumed his position standing at the drawing board, and said, "Where was I—?"

"Sorry about the interruption. At this rate, we'll never get anything done."

"Speak for yourself, Millie. I never allow anything to interfere with my devotion to duty. Oh yes, if we sell it, the drawing will be used on the can label and of course in television advertising—she'll come alive, but she'll look like the dead spit of your girl—so there ought to be quite a lot of money involved."

"I never work on speculation," Millie said firmly.

He gave her a wry smile. "I didn't think you did. How much?"

She felt a little off center, talking hardheadedly about money, work, with the man who had fed her and held her and lightly kissed her last night.

"For the ad alone, then, fifteen hundred dollars, and then we'll see about my fringe benefits in packaging and television."

He gave her a long, thoughtful look, the creases in his cheeks deepening into what might have been a smile.

"Funny, this being on two levels," he said, shorthand again, perhaps reading her mind. "Was that Mike Garland? I heard a syllable or two before— It's a bit more than I'd thought of paying, but of course you're worth it. I don't think I've seen you really rested before, Shattner or no Shattner. You might take off that wet cape now, you're looking very warm, delightfully. . . . How long do you think you'll take to do it? I'm told you're a very fast gun at your work. . . ."

She fought to keep herself quiet and direct and efficient, the accomplished and well-paid professional woman on, in one way, a perfectly normal assignment, out of town.

Frightfully egotistical, absurd, to think that he—sitting erect at his board, brown-and-white checked gingham shirt, sleeves turned up over the strong shapely forearms, gray eyes near, locked in hers, a well-made man, civilized and talented—that he had plainly been intended from birth for you. And you for him.

That had been, all too obviously, his girl, on the telephone. Oh . . . hi . . .

That had been Mike Garland, for her. I had to hear your voice.

"You've fallen into an almighty silence," Gus said. He leaned over and took her hand, put it on his board and covered it with his own, moving his long fine fingers a little over hers. "Not cold any more. In good working shape, I'd say. Or are you left-handed?"

"No, right-handed. . . . Oh, you asked how long." She removed her hand very lightly and casually and used it to brush a damp lock back from her forehead. "I don't know how long I'll be *here*, but of course I can finish it in New York if— In any case, unless I can't get to it at all, for some reason, two days, three. I'll have to browse around calicos and find the right rocker and polish up my cat anatomy. . . ."

"Well, if it isn't little Mrs. Jonas!" Ryan's hearty voice said from the door. "Welcome aboard—" He laughed at this and slapped his sides appreciatively. "No, rephrase that, James Thomas. Any word from the bonny boy?"

"No."

He came over and put a hand on her shoulder, beaming, paternal —almost.

She looked up into the pale green eyes that hadn't been informed about the big good-natured grin.

"Good girl, been to the police. I spent some time this morning—to be crude, about a hundred and fifty dollars' worth—with some earnest plodder, Detective Sergeant Something, wanting to know if he'd showed yet, and if he often disappeared like this, and—it's only fair to report to you, Mrs. Jonas dear—did I know anything about the wife, had this kind of thing happened before, her rushing here and thinking there was something wrong—"

His hand on her shoulder felt very hard, and very heavy. Gus watched and listened silently.

"I said, about you, 'Not to my knowledge, Captain'—it never does any harm to promote them, over the phone—and that as far as not showing up, unreliability is his secret weapon. He's like a drop of mercury, try to catch it with your finger—"

"You're wasted in advertising, Jim," Gus said, suddenly sounding for the first time Millie had heard him, deliberately landed gentry. "There's some broken-down ward, somewhere, that needs you, running for something and kissing babies and explaining hard real things away: 'Bless us all, it's nothing, my friends—'"

"Our polite neighborhood bastard," Ryan said to Millie. Voice making an attempt at banter, but a cold hostility underneath. "Sometimes I almost think he's not a dedicated member of the team. But good, by God, and well-connected too."

He gave Millie a final pressure of the shoulder before he dropped his hand.

"Am I interrupting a working session? It sort of looked like one. Have you hired the lady's services, Gus? Professionally, I mean, of course."

"Yes. I have, and you are."

Ryan turned to go. "I bet," he said, eyes musing on Millie, with her cape off now, and her soft gray suit lightly indicating her body, "she's expensive. Well, nice to have her decorating the premises, at any rate."

Into the silence, Gus said, "Sorry to expose you to this—and expose is the right word—but, you say you've met other Ryans."

"Yes, agencies are not exactly green woodlands full of lilies of the valley. How do *you* work with them, Gus? Those two? I mean, not just them, but their ideas, their whole approach. From what little I heard, they're not at all your style. Any more than," she smiled, "square dancing."

"I have an unfair and uncricket advantage," he said. "I don't really have to use it, it just sits there, looming at them. My cousin Farnall is chairman of the board of Guardian Petroleum. And a director of Friendship Foods. The two biggest accounts here. About seventeen million in all. And no, I didn't get my job here because of that. Alex Homans didn't even know it when he beckoned me here. It's a sort of coincidence of cousins."

He answered his telephone and told someone he couldn't have lunch, sorry, and went on:

"Naturally the New York agencies want Guardian and Friendship for themselves and keep sniping at them. But we Welcomes and Farnalls are fortunately a close-knit clan. To answer your question more specifically, about working with them, I do it their way and then I do it my way. And mostly my way is bought."

"You're lucky in your relatives. Brick town houses and board chairmen."

Farnall. Farnall? Where had she seen, or heard the name, or something like it, not very long ago?

Something to do with Jonas.

Better not press it, pursue it, or it would continue in hiding.

Ask the obvious question, though.

"Did, by any chance, Jonas know your cousin Farnall?"

"I don't think so. Augustus's—he uses it full blast—only connection with the rough and tumble of business in Philadelphia is a senior vice-president of the Girard Bank."

Amused by some recollection of his full-blast cousin, he said, "He lives in his place in Wayne and seldom emerges from it, devotes himself exclusively to the raising of a belatedly born four-year-old son, and orchids. A fearless murderer of quail and pheasants in their proper season, too."

Obviously at a far remove from Jonas's crass hustling world.

But that didn't erase the name, the tickle at her memory.

If she looked the other way, left it alone, it would surely come back to her.

Twelve

"Heavens, Olivia, are you in disguise?" Millie asked, looking at the unlikely white-blond wig.

Having none of her own equipment at hand, she had half arranged herself in an unoccupied windowless cubicle across the hall and up one door from Gus's office, where she would work, and then taken a cab to the Delancey Street house, to see Olivia and see what, if anything, had surfaced about Jonas.

"In a way, I am," Olivia said. "Lots of things to go into, but first sit down and have some coffee. My, you're wet." She had long been used to being taken for a lesbian, which she was not, and had defensively settled for a mildly bluff manner without verbal graces or decorations.

From the kitchen, she said, "Nothing in his mail but bills. He's still outrageously extravagant. A hundred and fifty pounds for a suit he ordered from London, and a fruiterer's bill, for God's sake, I didn't know there were fruiterers any more—"

She set a cup of coffee before Millie and went on, "I'm up to something in the bedroom—will you excuse me for a minute?" and disappeared again.

The telephone rang. Before Millie could even say hello, a relieved and rushing voice, young, female, private-school mannered, said:

"Jonas! Darling! I was so terrified when Aldy—that *bitch*, I'll fix him—"

"Jonas isn't here, I'm afraid," Millie said.

Olivia's wigged head poked out of the bedroom door.

"Who's that? Jonas?"

"Oh." The other voice taking breath, flattened. "Who are you?" Millie identified herself.

"But I thought *you* were sort of way back when," the girl said. "Are you why I can't reach him anywhere? Are you why everybody says he's not around?"

"No," Millie said. "No, I'm not. He has, at least for the moment, disappeared." Perhaps, from now on, dismiss tact, dismiss taste. "I thought he might be with you, if you're Amanda Graves."

"I am, but he isn't. I'm not in town, but—" A thoughtful pause. "Maybe I can find out where he is, if I—oh, sorry, won't keep you. Good-bye, Ms. Lester."

The reclosed bedroom door opened a crack. Olivia's hand came out. "Scissors around anywhere, Millie? I need scissors."

A hasty unhopeful search—what would Jonas be doing with a pair of scissors anyway?—yielded up red-handled kitchen shears in the drawer under the white counter beside the sink. Millie placed them in the large square hand.

Remembering as she did, Jonas saying, about Olivia, "Of course she doesn't like me. How would you feel if you were born first and looked on from infancy as a great stamping overgrown galumph, and then along comes a kid who happens to be a boy and looks just like you and everybody thinks he's the handsomest little charmer that ever drew breath?"

For comfort amid grotesqueries—the mysterious demand for the scissors, the fruiterer's bill, and "I thought you were way back when" —she sent her mind down Gus Welcome's stairway, past the blue and white room, the yellow room, into the tall living room that would breathe peace even in the heavy dark rain.

". . . *You're moving in under my eaves. . . .*" Move out, fast.

"Now then!" Olivia cried, flinging open the bedroom door and standing still and straight for inspection.

"Dear God." Millie's sudden movement sent the empty coffee cup to the rug, where it lay unbroken.

Jonas standing in Jonas's bedroom doorway. Olivia with her hair trimmed to Jonas's careless shining lion locks, wearing his cream flannel trousers, his moccasins, his raspberry red linen shirt, open at the throat. Jonas with breasts, not very showy ones, but—

Olivia interpreted the flicker in her stunned gaze and went and got his voluminous caped Burberry trenchcoat and put it on.

"—and that takes care of *those*," she said. "Good, isn't it? You look just right, Millie, as if you were seeing a ghost."

"What's it all about? What are you going to do with this—apparition?"

"I thought it up on the train coming here," Olivia said. "And I figured I'd play it by ear. I don't know quite how I'll use it yet, but for the first time looking like the wrong copy of my own brother might just turn out to be an advantage."

"Won't you be taking an awful chance if . . . somebody *has* done something to him?"

"Let's skip the euphemisms," Olivia said. "If, if. If somebody's done away with him, you mean, shot him, killed him. You seemed pretty sure of that when you talked to me on the phone. Have you any reason to think differently now?"

"No—I don't know. Now you see him, now you don't. A lot of things have happened since I talked to you—"

"Well, about taking a chance, here's the way I see it. If it's all, excuse me, a figment of your imagination, or if Jonas is off on something of his own and went underground on purpose, there's no harm done with me playing him. If someone has killed him they're going to get an awful turn, to say the least—a fainting spell or a foaming fit. But, you know, no point in their killing Jonas all *over* again. Don't you agree?"

What would it feel like, Millie wondered with an inward shudder. To turn a corner and see the man you thought you had killed, and disposed of, getting off a bus at the corner of Broad and Chestnut . . . or having a drink at the Barclay Bar . . . or strolling into the reception room at Homans?

"Now I'll get back into my own things. I don't want to tip my hand to anyone who might come knocking at the door."

She told herself that she didn't want any more Shattners or other Homans personnel inserting keys in the lock of the Bellevue suite. It was, however, the growing sense of obligation, involvement, a new danger that had nothing to do with Jonas, but with Gus Welcome, that sent her out into the thinning rain.

There was not another room to be had at the Bellevue, nothing at any of the large hotels. The motels were full. She had hit some kind of summit of conventions. She had to settle for a reasonably all-right room in a small hotel called the Garriston, on Locust Street.

She collected her bag from the suite and moved into her new quarters, mostly magenta, with shiny veneered surfaces of a clashing bright brown. What did it matter, a day or so . . . ?

Was that optimism or pessimism, thinking things would arrange themselves, reveal themselves, had to, soon, very soon? Surely she couldn't go on in this aimless groping way much longer. There was life to be resumed.

Olivia, in any case, would be looking for Jonas. Amanda Graves was looking for him, and the police were at least asking questions about him. And then there was the ad, which she had forgotten about until just now.

She called a messenger service to go to the offices of the three papers and pick up her mail—bring it to the Homans Agency around three, please—ate a sandwich and drank a cup of coffee at a drugstore counter up the street from the Garriston. Was Gus having lunch with his girl? He had told the telephone, after he had talked to her, that he was busy for lunch. . . .

She looked with great concentration at slices of raisin pound cake and Danish pastries on a plastic-shielded stand and encountered a feeling of having, in a way, lost herself.

When just three days ago she had been so sure, so able, so in control of her present, her future.

"I was more or less thinking of being married in July, or August—"

The statement seemed remote, unreal, somebody else's plans. Of course she wouldn't marry him. If even the first look at one man, standing in a station, waiting for her, could shake her so, marriage would be a kind of madness. She had chosen badly before. Perhaps she was blindly, obsessively doing it again—

She drew sharply back from making any kind of decision, right now. She wasn't herself, her aloneness accessoried by cake stands and a neon Coca-Cola sign facing her and the remains of weak coffee in a thick cup, the rim so worn with wear and washing and other people's mouths that it rasped the skin of her lips.

"Millie, are you crazy?" Gus said. "Don't you know all those places are firetraps? God knows who's in the next room, drunk, the mattress about to go up. Walking out of a nice comfortable setup at the Bellevue—Shattner certainly won't try anything again. We had a few sharp short words this morning—"

He sounded like an irate husband.

Millie said soothingly, "It's highly temporary. I can chance it for a night or so, it doesn't look that bad. . . ." And then, business, yes. "Is there anyone I can borrow, a secretary, a typist, to sit in a chair for me so I can begin to lay in your calico girl?"

She sat at her board. He stood leaning against the wall opposite, glaring at her.

"Yes, you can have mine in a minute . . . but *why*, Millie?"

"I like to work from life when I can—"

"I don't mean why the model. Why are you saying thanks but no thanks to the perfectly good accommodations you've been provided with?"

A little desperately, she said, "I don't want to keep asking favors, attentions, having people feel they have to drop everything— And I owe you far too much already."

"You don't owe me anything." He thrust his hands into his pockets and stood looking down into her eyes. " 'I was thinking of being married in July. . . .' Were you afraid I'd use *my* key in your door? Tonight, maybe?"

"As a matter of fact, that never occurred to me. . . ."

"I don't know why not," Gus said, and then something shadowed his face a little. He added abruptly, "But I'm holding you up. I'll go get Robin for you."

Robin posed patiently, holding in her lap a cat-sized crush of paper from the drawing pad. She was a pretty, gangly girl in her early twenties, with the Philadelphia cockney accent that identified her origins and background inexorably.

"Tell me when you're tired."

"I will, I'm used to this—Gus, Mr. Welcome, often wants a hand or a leg, or a foot."

"You make him sound like a cannibal. . . . Is he nice to work for?"

"Best job in the place," Robin said. "Or we girls say so anyway. He's so, well, darling-looking, and he can be funny, too—sometimes he kills me. And he couldn't care less if you have to go out in the afternoon to pick up a pair of shoes, or leave early to have your hair done. . . . That Shattner, now, he's strictly bad news." She managed to get an *a*, an *i*, and an *o* into the word *news*. "The next best bet to Gus would be I'd say Jonas. . . . We heard you were—I mean you once were—" As she spoke Jonas's name she gave a pleased giggle. "He could be *nutty*—you know?—but in a nice way. Once he sent every girl in the whole office a dozen white roses. You should have seen the boxes stacked up in the reception room—"

Millie worked, listening, garnering. Shattner's wife was rich, ordered him around. "And she comes in here once a week or so, inspecting things, and stares at everybody, particularly if a girl has on something sheer, or not wearing a bra. I don't know what she's worried about—the only thing he ever says to the girls is, 'Why can't you put your makeup on at home and not on company time,' or, 'What the hell do you think you're being paid for, a nine-to-five coffee break—?'"

Ryan, now—he liked girls. Don't get caught alone with him in the Xerox room. Not that he'd *do* anything; he had his reputation to look out for. They said he was going to be president—and of course he had a wife and kids—

But he'd say things . . . and look at you in a way that, well, *you* know?

Not like Jonas, not like Gus. They were men, real men, but they didn't make you feel funny.

But maybe Ryan, in spite of the remarks he passed, was better than Aldington. "He's in and out of here a lot, treats we girls like dirt. Please fetch me some coffee, he says. *Fetch*. And he's cold, he makes you feel as if your blood had all drained out of you. . . ."

A girl stopped in the doorway of the cubicle.

"Hello, Robin. Gus around? Yes, I agree with you about Aldington . . ." laughing, "but you should be careful. I heard your analysis four doors down, and you know his impulsive temper—"

She had a lazy, pretty voice. She was tall, belted into a trenchcoat, and gypsy dark and rose-colored. She gave Millie a light, thoughtful, and thorough look.

"In a meeting, Virginia. Want to wait for him? He said four, and it's just about that now—"

"When he says four he means four," Gus said, from behind the dark girl. She swung radiantly to him. Over her head, his eyes met Millie's, and then he lowered the timeless strange gaze to the girl's face.

"Darling," she said, "happy birthday. I just got back from New York. I couldn't wait to—"

"Don't breathe another word or someone will go out and buy a cake. Robin, you didn't hear it."

And then there was—a vast relief—nothing to have to hear, after his office door was quietly closed.

Well, that takes care of that, Millie informed herself in an odd kind of calm.

Gus Welcome's wide door. Shut.

Thirteen

Almost on cue with the closing door, the telephone pulled her back out of his life and into her own.

A woman's voice, businesslike. A Helen Horner of Horner Realtors. "Mrs. Rath? Or, you were—sorry, a bit confused. I don't like to bother you at work, but there's some very odd woman at Mr. Rath's apartment. Refused to say where he was, and why did I want to know, and then said she couldn't discuss real estate matters without a lawyer present, and that I should call you—"

"Yes, what is it?" Millie smiled at the patient Robin and waved a thanking, dismissing hand to her.

It seemed that Jonas had been contemplating buying a house in Society Hill. "Marvelous condition, vintage fireplaces, pearwood paneling in the library. . . ." Helen Horner went on about the charms of the house as if she thought Millie might be a possible purchaser if Jonas didn't, after all, want it.

"Yes, it sounds lovely, but he's not around just now—"

"The real point of my call is the key," the woman said briskly. "I must have it back. He's such a sweet man, but, you know, I get the impression he's a little careless. And he's had it now, what, two, three days. I gave it to him late in the day on—let me check my calendar—yes, Monday, June first. He said he wanted to show some friends over the house."

Late in the day. June first. It was early in the morning on the second when he had called, when—

The sound crashed reverberating through her head again.

"Are you still there, Mrs. Rath?"

"Yes." In the few seconds, her mind had covered miles and turned a dozen frightening corners.

Have to, *have to* . . .

"As a matter of fact, he said he wouldn't make up his mind until I gave him my opinion on it." She was amazed at the cool authority in her own voice. "I suppose you have another key? I could stop by for it quite soon."

"Yes, of course, but I can't take you through myself. I have several people waiting here who—"

"That's perfectly all right." She jotted the address of Horner Realtors on her drawing pad.

A missing man. An empty house, to which he had a key that he had been expected to return. He might be hiding there from something, or somebody.

It suddenly seemed a reasonable explanation for everything.

She closed the box of watercolors she had borrowed from Gus, snapped off the light in the cubicle, and, pulling on her cape, went out into the reception room.

The girl at the switchboard gave a guilty start at the sight of her.

"I could kill myself, Ms. Lester. Some mail came for you by messenger a while ago and then this board blew up in my face, and I forgot all about it—" She handed Millie envelopes in a rubber band. "I hope it was nothing urgent."

She ripped open and read one of the answers to her ad in the elevator going down sixteen floors. A slippery piece of photocopy paper from what seemed to be a quasi-religious organization calling itself the Truth-Seekers. ". . . learn our processes of prayer and meditation and you will seek and find your loved ones and rejoice in their constant presence. Ten dollars for 12 issues of our inspirational magazine. . . ."

Continuing to tear open envelopes and trying to signal a cab didn't, she found, work together. It would all probably be hopeless crank stuff anyway.

Going east on Chestnut Street in a taxi which no longer offered springs in its back seat, she read two more of the letters.

"Dear Millie R., I may not be Jonas R., but let me list my attractions for you—" Obscenities, the handwriting a brutal scrawl, half leaning forward, half backward. Revolted, she crumpled it and hurled it out of the open window beside her. The long-haired jeaned boy at the wheel giggled and said, "You're littering, ma'am."

A form letter from a private detective agency. ". . . highest quality personnel, many retired police officers, utmost discretion assured to you . . ."

They turned south into Eighth Street and over to Pine. Horner Realtors was one flight up, over a pleasant-looking shop selling antiques and curiosities.

Helen Horner, an untied-looking bundle of a woman, gave her the key and said, "You sounded all right and you *look* all right. I normally wouldn't—but of course if he has to have your opinion, I suppose that's what the holdup has been. Please do return it. If I'm not here you can just drop it in through the mail slot—"

It was an unsuitable afternoon to have a nightmare in. Mysterious and soft, the rain having removed itself but suggesting its return in a silvered lavender light.

And an attractive unlikely place.

She had heard and read about Society Hill, taking its name from the Free Society of Traders, and saw that it was not really a hill at all but a long, almost imperceptible, slope to—what?—yes, the Delaware River. An urban redevelopment area which had turned out to be a dazzling success. Living there so felicitous, fresh and free and open and gardeny, that more and more big money was crowding in, threatening to bleed some of its fabled beauties to death.

She was passing old Pine Street Church, a fine honey yellow, white columned and balconied and pedimented, when she felt a strange tickle at the back of her neck. She stopped and took off her shoe as though looking for a pebble in it, and turned her head.

The shabby little man was perhaps fifteen feet behind her on the otherwise empty pavement. He had stopped, too.

She was tired of being adrift and at the mercy of unseen forces. She remembered thinking furiously, I'm sick of mystery. She put on her shoe and ran straight at him.

He slipped through the open gate in the iron railing. A wedding party just coming out of the church gazed with astonishment at the sight of a young woman in a red cape chasing a small elderly man through the gravestones.

She caught up with him easily and clutched his arm and backed him up against a tall stone. She had no fear of him, up close.

Broken teeth, watery gray eyes, mouth shaking in fear as he struggled under her grip. He steamed whiskey at her.

"Let me go, you've got no right to grab me—"

"Why are you following me?" Millie demanded. "Who are you working for?"

"Ain't following you. Leave me go—"

She lifted a hand and struck his face, hard, overtaken by a sort of savagery she hadn't known her nature held.

"Who is it? Who pays you to follow me?"

She felt him trembling.

"Mr. Rath, then." Voice something between a wail and a choke. "Leave me go—Mr. Jonas Rath."

"How do you get your orders from him? Where do you see him?"

"Over the phone—I never seen him. He leaves my pay at a newsstand on Market Street and I leave my report there for him. You're hurting my arm—"

A young man with the look of a curate approached. "Is there any —are you in any trouble?" he asked, looking from her to the abject little man.

"Not real trouble, I don't think. This man has been following me and he's to stop. The next time I see him I will hand him over to the police, but this time . . ."

She felt a sort of indecency at further terrifying this tired, used, frightened man.

"I won't, miss—the hell with it. It's not all that much money anyway. . . ."

"I will escort him to the street and say a word or so to him on the way," the curate said. "You're sure you're all right? You look—"

"I am, thank you—yes, I think I am," Millie said. "I'll just . . . lean here for a minute. . . ." The worn stone was reassuringly hard and cool against her cheek.

"I can get you a cup of tea. . . ."

"No, all I want is a moment or so, and then I'll be on my way."

Don't think about it, or ponder on it, or at least not until you get away from all these gravestones.

With a summoned and unnatural calm, she did think about it, as she walked.

Well, of course. Whoever it was would tell him to say it was Jonas if he got caught. Quite a good idea, when you thought about it, because the little man, over the phone, wouldn't know, and she had no way of proving it wasn't . . .

But, yes, that was it. Of course.

The foursquare Dutch-gabled tapestry brick house that Jonas had been thinking of buying stood on a still-enchanting unflawed block. Walking slowly and a little unwillingly toward it, she was aware of the sweet silence in the silvered air. A silence underlined by the curiously personal sound of one hammer, somewhere near, driving in one nail. The street was cobblestoned, the sidewalk herringbone-bricked. Strange to think that all this was just fourteen blocks away from clamoring Broad Street and the nerve center of the city.

A carillon began a sleepy hymn. A linden tree, diamonded with water, moved in a breeze over her head. Not far away, I. M. Pei's three towers stood, tall, solemn, separate. Yellow roses poured over a garden wall, and in a young round maple tree, celebrating June with its greenness, an oriole uttered a scale of golden notes. From some open window there floated a smell of bread baking.

Under other circumstances, it would have induced a sense of great peace.

The house looked very large, its uncurtained windows very blank and dark. What had seemed, in the offices of Homans, a clearcut necessity now took on the air of a hazardous venture. Taking the telephone call, she had not thought Jonas's expedition into real estate particularly odd. He had always been full of schemes—escape hatches, he called them.

Let's start a sable farm, Millie—rich men's rats. Or, what about a marina . . . a country inn? . . . Let's cash in on the art racket, open a gallery, you the brains and me the gall and the charm. . . .

Now face to face with the house, she was given severe pause. On receiving the key, she had asked about the price and had been told, casually, one hundred and thirty-five thousand and a giveaway at that.

Helen Horner added, "I'll be glad to give you the grand tour through it tomorrow and point out all the treasures, but if you insist on a preliminary view, do go ahead."

Where would Jonas get the money for a down payment on such a sum? Amanda? Granted his large salary as a consultant, he would probably be living up to every penny of it and well beyond.

". . . I also have the feeling that Jonas has something on one or the other of the unholy pair. . . ." Gus, talking about Ryan and Shattner.

An ugly picture beginning to form itself—or perhaps it had been there all the time, subsurface, unexamined—the child's chant, forefinger signaling, at right angles to the other forefinger, ". . . what I know about *you!*"

Fourteen

She was suddenly aware that she still held one unopened letter in her left hand.

Knowing that she was deliberately putting off something that must be done, she sat down on a white marble step and applied herself to the envelope.

It held a folded sheet of white bond paper. On it was scrawled in Jonas's large, black, unmistakable hand, "Go to hell."

She refolded it, put it carefully into her handbag, walked up the marble steps and put the key in the door, and turned it. An absolute sort of emptiness came at her, a thick-walled house on a quiet cobblestoned street with nobody, surely nobody in it. Semi-dark except where cool silver shone through the panes onto the highly waxed floors.

She looked at, without seeing it, the square white entrance hall, the long splendid room to the right of it.

It was—the note—shocking, sickening, but at first impact it felt wrong. If Jonas wanted to insult you on paper, he was usually a good deal more stylish about it. He would never, as she knew him, resort to this brutal shout. But she didn't know him any more, hadn't known him for two years.

Dining room to her left, and then a huge kitchen floored in red Spanish tiles. The kitchen was being worked on, perhaps by nonunion after-hours men. There was a stack of white, brown-veined marble slabs near a long counter with its top missing, an empty paper cup on top of the stack, a telephone on the floor—

A telephone.

She looked from it back to his "Go to hell."

Now was not the time to let any power of thought, of judgment, slip away and leave her naked, an object against which things washed and broke and had their will like restless untidy surf.

Think. Think. If a curt unknown Jonas hadn't sent this to her, who had?

Conceivably, someone had written some comment or criticism or directive on a memo of Jonas's—someone at Homans. And this had been his contemptuous answer to the writer.

Why send it in response to her ad? A malicious whim on someone's part? Like Aldington's "a dog named Jonas?"

An attempt, perhaps, to add another handful of mist to the cloudy legend that it was all a mistake, a wild goose chase, that Jonas was still very much alive. So go home, Millie. Forget it.

Or it could be Jonas himself, saying to her, Get out, leave me alone. You're not my wife any more, keep out of my business. Go to hell. The roughest, quickest, and most final sort of command, to get her off his back for once and all.

She turned and left the kitchen and went up the broad stairs from the entrance hall and blankly inspected three commodious bedrooms. One of the bedrooms was in the process of being painted a pale lemon yellow. How could he be hiding here if workmen were coming in and out? Unless they worked desultorily, on weekends—or maybe he had handed around a few five-dollar bills.

Someone was, or had been, making use of the bathroom off the lemon bedroom. A roll of toilet paper informally planted on the floor, a dirty thin white towel over the rack, the toilet seat up, a smeared cake of pink soap on the sink. No, never—he was as clean as a cat. Never.

She went back to the kitchen. The counter with its top off looked like a tremendous coffin. Tiptoeing, body shrinking back, head thrust forward, she made herself peer in. Darkness, dust, plumbing. To the right of the counter was a door. She opened it and felt the cold coming up from what must be old cavernous cellars, black. A scuttling, rustling sound down there, probably a rat. Of course, a rat—

No power on earth could draw her down into those cellars.

Her head felt peculiar. Perhaps she was getting a little dotty.

Obsessed. Reading mysteries into ordinary faces, natural events, and perfectly respectable houses. Feeding her own guilt about not having answered that first call, when there might have been some way she could have helped him, forestalled whatever had happened. *If* he had needed help, *if* something had happened. If it wasn't all a fantasy of hers—

. . . My dear, have you encountered that *pathetic* Lester woman? She's been wandering around for days, weeks—*years?*—looking for some man she used to be married to. . . . She rambles on and on about some crazy phone call. . . . I understand she used to be quite attractive, and successful, you know, and on the brink of getting married to . . .

She felt suddenly faint, and ill, and very much tempted to start screaming into the silence of the tapestry brick house.

Fifteen

It was a bad time in the white hall, a doorknob just a few inches from her hand, waiting to let her out, into the world—a very bad time.

She had had her share of crises and recognized the danger, close, of panicking. Cracking and crumbling under the pressure. A small clear voice in the back of her mind began to give her instructions. She followed them humbly.

First she went back to the kitchen, picked up the telephone, called Helen Horner and said there were sounds in the cellars, possibly only mice but perhaps rats, but she must, tomorrow, see the cellars. Could an exterminator or some helpful man look them over before she made her descent? Yes, she would keep the key until the following morning.

Then she went out into the evening, overclouded now, a dark violet color. Walk hard. Turn yourself outward. Observe the world around you closely. Give your mind a chance to breathe quietly and rest.

Fast striding took her across to Chestnut and up.

She summoned painful attention, read plaques. *Pemberton House, Army-Navy Museum, 1775–1805. Second Bank of the United States*— noble pillars and pediments pocked and textured with time—*erected 1819–1824. Designed by William Strickland.*

Independence Hall. She'd been taken there when she was seven and remembered nothing of it. Beyond, on the corner of Sixth and Chestnut, Congress Hall. Inside, an angled white staircase going up right against the windowpanes. *Capitol of the United States*

1790–1800. Here the Senate and House of Representatives met during the nation's formative years. Here George Washington was inaugurated for a second term as president in 1793; John Adams took his oath here in 1797. Library Hall, American Philosophical Society. Benjamin Franklin high in a marble niche.

She turned in to the cobblestoned walk at the side of Library Hall. Brick silences, green silences. With an air of great purpose, she continued her exploration. The statue over there to her right, near Walnut? Robert Morris.

She crossed more cobblestones. Fifth Street. The grass had been mowed not long ago and the air was soaked with a green fragrance. The white-belfried dark brick was Carpenters' Hall. *Meeting place of the First Continental Congress in 1774 . . . erected in 1770.*

Back over to Walnut and down. She saw, through black iron rails, a garden which looked like a work of embroidery. She thought it was a public garden. It was.

On the tilted board just inside its entrance: *You are standing on the spot of "a garden on Walnut Street," so described in 1784. The present garden illustrates several aspects of Philadelphia gardening, with its walks, small orchard, geometrically patterned flower beds and gazebo. The trees, shrubs, and flowers are all species known to have grown in Philadelphia before 1800.*

The garden was deserted. She walked the gravel paths between orderly beds of ageratum and roses and geraniums. At the rear of the garden, the arborlike latticed gazebo poured grapevines. Beyond that, on soft rich grass, young apple and plum trees were neatly spaced. There wasn't a sound, except for a sleepy cheep from a nest in one of the apple trees.

Millie bathed herself in the silent garden. Stood regarding the primly rounded trees of yellow lantana. Bent to sniff a pale pink rose, the old-fashioned kind with winy spice and lemon under its rich rose sweetness.

There was a crunch on the gravel behind her. She turned without fear, knowing in her blood who it was.

Gus gave her face a lengthy and anxious examination. "What's the matter, Millie? I mean right now?"

Having at least partially escaped a great danger, and not wanting right now to turn around and stare it in the face again, she asked, "How on earth did you find me?"

"With a great deal of trouble," he said patiently. "I looked for you in your little hole and you'd gone. I called Olivia and the only help she had to give was to say artists tended to be irresponsible, didn't I find? Then your answering service attacked. Mike Garland wanted you—twice—from Rome. And someone at CBS has what he described as a juicy job for you—"

"God, I keep messing up your schedule," Millie said. "I'm sorry, but I still don't see how—"

"I found the scribble on your pad, the real estate people, and after calling on them and pounding on the door of the tapestry brick, I just began driving around. And there you were, with your face in a rosebush."

"I wouldn't blame you for sharing my own opinion that I'm going slightly out of my mind—"

"On the contrary," he said. "You're such a rational woman I didn't understand your darting off like that, without notice, and I was frightened as hell about you."

Rational. The word fell on her ear like a sweet blessing.

He saw the tears in her eyes, her face white, almost blue, in the dimming garden. He reached for her hand and led her in under the sheltering arbor and took her in his arms. His kiss was not quick and lightly tasting, as before, but claiming and passionate.

Let it go, let everything go. This is all, really, that matters. Nothing else means a damned thing—

Mike Garland wanted you twice from Rome.

Isn't this maybe Jonas all over again? Isn't this why you divorced him? Off with the old, on with the new. I want him, why shouldn't I have him? Let other people pick up the pieces—

Happy birthday, darling. . . .

He hardly heard what she said, her face buried against him. ". . . ought to be getting back to your birthday party . . ."

"You're my birthday party." He kissed her again before she could move away.

". . . not only ruining your workday, but your—that pretty dark girl—"

He took his arms away and put his hands on her shoulders and looked hard at her. "I haven't taken any vows," he said. "Have you?— I did once, and after a while it didn't work, and we were divorced, just about when you were. And I've been fairly prudent since then, but there comes a time when to be—oh, everyday loyal, decent, is a sort of madness. Particularly when it's your whole life—"

"A sort of madness . . ." she repeated, murmuring. "I used to think I could separate things. . . ."

She picked up his hand and kissed it.

"Are you giving something back to me, Millie?"

"Yes, in a way." She hadn't known until now that her mind had been making itself up, somewhere in the empty house, or on her sightseeing walk through bricks and grass and cobblestones. "I'm going back to New York tomorrow. I can't stay here any longer. I'm coming all . . . loose from my moorings. I don't know what's real any more and what's false, fake—"

"Mike Garland being your moorings?" She hadn't thought a face as handsomely skeptical could look, for a moment, so savage.

"A part of them, I suppose. I have to warn you—when you asked what's the matter—a short time ago in a nice big empty house for sale, I almost flipped. I'd heard the word but not the music. I'm in no condition to—" She put both hands to her face.

There was a long silence from him. Then he said, "All right, Gus, there's a strong possibility that after all you're false and you're fake. For Christ's sake get off Millie's grass. Yes, go back to New York, sensible of you. You've done all you can do here—I'll buy you a farewell drink. I think I need one." Some of the hard, hurt rage went out of his voice. He added, "You're in no danger, now, in my company. Nor I in yours. I'm an illusion. Probably you are, too."

They walked silently out of the garden. Millie's very bones ached as though she had expended all her bodily strength in some impossible exercise. Giving Gus Welcome away.

After a few moments she couldn't bear his stillness. "Tell me about some of these lovely things we're walking past. I probably won't see them again."

"To your left, St. Paul's Church. It was built with funds raised by a lottery, which didn't seem to trouble anyone in those days, 1760 or so. On your right—" his voice light and amiable, seeming to come from very far away—"Powel House, with one *l*. Washington and Lafayette dropped in. Built in 1765. Up ahead here, the Bouvier houses. Funny to see brownstone in all this brick. Michel Bouvier, the lady's great-great-grandfather, bought them in 1849. Approaching Head House Square. Used to be an open-air market for a century or so. All restored and rebuilt now, or most of it. Immediately to your right, a drink."

They went into a conscientious attempt at a reproduction of an English pub. Two girls giggled at a corner table. A man at the bar sipped beer and rustled a newspaper. The light was dim and warm. Millie said she would like a martini, please. "Two," Gus said to the waitress.

They touched glasses politely. She said, "I can't leave those words in your mouth—fake, false, illusion—if I don't see you again. I was talking about what's been happening to me, about Jonas, about you, about everybody. I'm not going to tell you about this afternoon, because you'd think I'm as mad as I thought I was. There was someone —harmless, really—a man, shaking with fear, and I struck him in the face. He was just trying to make a little money. His clothes were so shabby but trying to be brushed and neat—" The distress in her voice told him not to pursue this matter further, just now. "I'm turning into a dish of pudding, but do forgive me. You've been so very kind to me, so good, and—"

He was looking into his glass, not at her. As she fumbled the words out, she studied his face, trying to memorize it, the mouth, the brow, the angles of the cheekbones.

To the tabletop, he said, "Do what you think best for yourself. At least for the time being. By the way, I am not a charitable institution, dispensing kindness and goodness to all comers. In my case it's purely selfish and personal. The thing you're going to have to face, Millie, is that you may never know what happened to him. I hope it's not going to obsess you. Probably the saner course would be to decide he chose to disappear for some reason of his own and scrub the whole thing."

He raised his eyes to her and for a few startled seconds, taken unaware, they lost themselves, in delight, in each other.

The waitress, hovering, planted her hands on the table and beamed at them. "When's it to be?" she asked. "It's none of my business, but I like to see people in love—really in love, I mean. You don't see a lot of it these days. You wouldn't think it to look at me, stout and all, but I have it too, my Joe and me—Joe's my husband, eight years—so I know."

Gus took his eyes from Millie's rose-lighted stricken face and smiled at the waitress. "On that," he said, "we'll all three have a drink. Ours is in a hurry, I'm afraid, so bring along the check while you're about it."

Sixteen

"Black is the color of my true love's house," sang Amanda Graves as Aldington opened the front door to her triple ring.

He looked at her coldly. The overhead light in his hall exaggerated the deep lines from nose to mouth corners, the shadows under his pale eyes.

"And what tiles are you fresh from?" he asked. "Three days. Not a word."

"I love you in that light. You look dissolute and sort of evil. My scary Aldy." She hugged him around the waist and lifted her face. He gave her a small kiss on her forehead.

She followed him into the living room and threw herself into a red leather chair. The room, not accidentally, could have been lifted whole from one of the better men's clubs. Leather and books, formally looped and draped and pelmeted red velvet at the windows, a great carved oak fireplace with a wardrobe of shining brass fittings, a mahogany table holding French, English, and American periodicals, a comfortably ugly liver-red and dark green checked rug.

Amanda, in her jeans and loose raffish black turtleneck jersey, looked entirely out of place.

Aldington went to a corner table and mixed himself a strong scotch and soda. "Anything for you?"

"Ginger ale . . . I'm a bit adrift. . . ."

"Yes, I noticed."

"Don't be chilly," she said. "Mummy and I spent hours this morning, discussing wedding things, wondering what would be the most fun—"

"Indeed?" Aldington asked, still sulking. "Everybody unclothed? A mountaintop ceremony?"

"Oh, shut up, Aldy. You don't have to remind everyone that you're thirty-five. Give me a drink after all. Sherry, if you have it— the sweet stuff, not the dry."

He poured it with distaste and handed it to her. She drank and then deliberately and vulgarly smacked her lips. "I take it back, a little. Thirty-five's sort of young to be sort of famous like you are. And you can keep up scolding and frowning, because otherwise you wouldn't be my dear old cozy father figure, and it wouldn't work at all, would it?"

"It's your turn to shut up," Aldington said. He lifted her out of her chair and kissed her hard. Amanda responded and then slipped back and away from him just when his eyes began burning into hers.

"Filthy little cheat," Aldington said lightly, not going to let her have her malicious triumph. "Perhaps that's what I like in you. Don't you ever change for the better, either."

"I'm not cheating," Amanda said. "It's just that we have to talk seriously for a little while, and after that we can play. Get me another sherry and sit down."

Not liking to be given orders, he filled her glass and then took a considerable time getting his pipe lighted, puffed at it for a few moments, and finally sat down on the arm of the sofa across from her chair, swinging one leg.

Amanda's eyes sparkled. "There's one thing I want you to do for me before we have a nice reunion and discuss marriage plans. Find Jonas Rath."

Aldington took his pipe out of his mouth and gazed at the stem.

"You're joshing," he said. It was one of his Aldington things that he said on his show, to people with whom he coldly disagreed. It was always meant as a snub.

"I'm not. I heard you this morning. A dog named Jonas. He happens to be a friend of mine. You happen to be in what they call the communications business. Well, communicate around and find out where Jonas is."

"I will not only not do it, I will not be threatened," Aldington said, looking genuinely dangerous. "Is this an exercise? Are you sure you haven't just left his bed? His ex wife seemed to think the two of you might have been together— Or are we starting a fun-fun paper chase for all your bedmates?"

"Cut it out," Amanda said. "I don't fuss about all the women you've been to bed with. Unless you find him, we're not announcing anything. In fact, we're not even planning anything."

Aldington's chosen role was to correct, enlighten, and if necessary —and he found it often was—punish people. Permissive educators, unruly youth: "If only manufacturers would stop making blue *jeans* we might have a polite and civilized world again—" The vanishing race of servants: "It is a plain and simple fact that there is a good deal more honor and dignity, to say nothing of pleasant surroundings, in being an excellent lady's maid or gentleman's valet than in shuffling nameless objects on an assembly line in a dirty factory—" Idle tippling housewives: "The hand that reaches for the noon martini pitcher rocks the cradle and rules the world, God help us all—"

He was scarlet with rage at the whip of punishment used heavily and mercilessly across his own back.

"If I find him," he said in a silken tone, "I presume it won't matter whether he's alive or dead. Just that, like Everest, he's *there?*"

"Don't be ghoulish, Aldy," Amanda said, knowing what he was feeling, trying not to be too open about her enjoyment of it. "And it's just for old time's sake. I want him found, period. And then I promise I'll give him back for good to all his other girls."

Dora Maunder was feeling badly left out of things. It had all started out so thrillingly, just yesterday, the Jonas affair. There had been a sense of involvement in the air, comings and goings, discoveries. There had been the exciting if exhausting hunt for Jonas's car. And Gus Welcome's always eagerly listened-for voice, a different pitch than she remembered it, talking to Millie, overheard from her terrace. And Millie, so attractive, so interested in her, Dora's, information—

Now it had all stopped. She wasn't being asked to help, to do anything. It was apparent that she was not immediately wanted. If at all.

Very daring, she had stopped fighting temptation earlier in the af-

ternoon and slipped quietly up Jonas's stairway and with the greatest
caution peered in at the edge of the window. If caught, she'd say she
wanted to borrow sugar, or salt.

She saw Olivia sitting on the floor, her back to the window, sort-
ing through a sea of papers, now strewn all over the Bokhara carpet.
Hunting for his last will and testament or something? Or maybe an
uncashed check. Jonas often drove Payroll crazy at Homans by forgetting for weeks on end to cash his salary checks. Piled-up bills didn't
bother him at all, and he had every kind of credit card for daily ne-
cessities.

Well, Olivia, at this point, would be better than nothing. Move,
Dora, she said to herself. Things don't just happen, *people* make
them happen. Usher yourself right back in to the business of Jonas.
She fingered the gold fleur-de-lis bracelet. It gave her courage to go to
the telephone.

"Miss Rath? Dora Maunder, a next-door neighbor, an old friend
of Jonas's. Millie and I had a long talk when she got here and of
course I'm a bit worried, and wondering—has anyone heard from
him yet?"

"No," Olivia said, and asked bluntly, "Have you any idea of who'd
want to do away with him? Or whether he's running and hiding
from someone?"

"No, I haven't a clue, but I'm sure he's all right. I'm sure it's
just—"

"Just what?"

"Oh, a puzzlement," Dora said gaily. It was much more reassuring, much more intriguing, looked at that way.

"I hope you're right. I have a business to run and I can't spare
much more time, and Millie's informed me that *she's* going back to
New York tomorrow. Does he often disappear like this?"

"He went off a lot to Vermont in early spring, skiing, and didn't
leave a number where he could be reached in case Ryan or Shattner
wanted him, but other than that—"

"If this is a wild goose chase," Olivia said grimly, "—if he's
disporting himself on a beach somewhere, I'll gladly kill him myself.
Once he went to Switzerland when he was presumably due in

Chicago for a job interview. He said he got on the wrong plane. Well, thank you for your interest, Miss Maunder."

Dora went back to her couch and her drink, trying not to listen to the silence, the emptiness, around her. With Millie gone away, Olivia going, the whole matter apparently to be dropped, she would be back in the desert of her home vacation. The only thing to look forward to, a family weekend with Ellen and Joe at the shore, which Ellen was perfectly capable of canceling the day before.

Oh, Dora, I'm so sorry, but a little chum of Jessica's—or an old school buddy of Joe's—or an old friend of mine—has showed up unexpectedly and we'll need the room after all. Would next weekend be just as good for you? Or maybe midweek, when we're quiet and not partying around so much . . .

There was still tonight. But what action could be taken tonight?

And then, tomorrow, there would be nothing in her life. Absolutely nothing.

Uncannily, Aldington called her two minutes later.

"Miss Maunder? Kenneth Aldington."

So that was his name. She prepared to bristle. Perhaps he was going to pursue the matter of her arrest for trespassing.

His voice was uncharacteristically smooth and pleasant. "I'm afraid I was a bit brisk with you last evening. You gave me a fright, you know. I've been burgled twice in that house, both times with the entrance made from the garden."

"It's all right, of course I understand," flattered, now, "it was sweet of you to call—"

"And did you find your cat? Or rather your sister's cat?"

On guard again, Dora felt that he was about to grill her, find out that the cat was a fiction, and mete out punishment.

She said nervously, "No—yes, rather. I didn't find it, but it turned up and mewed at the window a little later. I won't keep you, Mr. Aldington."

"Actually, I had another reason for calling you. I understand you're very eager to get in touch with Jonas Rath. And I also gather there's been some suggestion of foul play in connection with him and his possible disappearance." How professionally he spoke, Dora thought. No ah's and er's and mm's, as if he was on the air.

"Yes, I am. I don't know if you heard—" No, don't continue on the eavesdropping theme. "His wife, his ex wife, thinks he might have been shot."

"When? When did she think this happened?"

"Let's see—late Monday, it would have been, after midnight, which would"—Dora found herself aping Aldington's precision—"which would then of course make it Tuesday."

"It so happens I may be able to help you. In fact, this little matter's been niggling at the edge of my mind. But you know how it is, one is frantically busy with one's own affairs. And anyway, I believe shooting is a commonplace in Philadelphia, the most respectable instances of it being police after fleeing burglars, one imagines. However—"

He paused. He sounded as if he was pulling on a pipe.

"I was at a party on Monday night. Do you know Blenheim Court? Not very fashionable, I'm afraid, but a few brave souls have started rather an exclusive little enclave there, and the neighborhood may take a turn for the better."

Dora scanned a mental map. "Yes, I think I sort of know where it is. Way south . . . near the river . . ."

"I believe the next street over—more an alley, I suppose—is called Trunk Street. Interesting name. One wonders . . . There was a Nathaniel Trunk who designed and built stagecoaches. . . ."

Dora's grip on the phone was damp. She waited.

"There are the usual back gardens in between the two streets, or in some cases small cement areas tastefully furnished with old automobile bodies, bedsprings, packing crates, and such things, as well as a good deal of burdock and ragweed, although my host's garden was quite a pleasant one. I was in the garden window more or less in the time area you mention, trying to find some air. I assume you're still on the line?"

"Yes—"

"I did think I heard something that sounded remarkably like a shot from one of the houses on Trunk Street, the one backing on my host's, or the one to the right or left of it, or perhaps across the alley, it's hard to say. There was a good deal of noise in the room behind me, and there was a bus accelerating nearby. I waited, you know, listening for the usual police sounds—sirens, commotion, shouts—and there was absolutely nothing."

"And what did you do then?" Dora asked breathlessly.

"Not a thing, my dear Miss Maunder. It was high time for another drink and, as I say, these outbursts are somewhat of a commonplace. But the circumstances were just the smallest bit peculiar."

Another interval of pipe-puffing.

"Oh, dear, I forgot to say that earlier in the course of the party the liquor began to run low, and I thought to augment the supply. I went to a state store which by some rare mad convenience is right at the end of Blenheim Court. Jonas was there, buying, I believe, champagne. I asked him with some considerable apprehension if he was on his way to *my* party, and he said no, he was going around the corner. Presumably into Trunk Street. Strange coincidence. An odd part of town to meet in. There are *people* there, of course, but not persons. Now there's my little titbit for you. I don't know what you'll do with it, but I just thought I'd pass it along. The party house, by the way, was about mid-block on Blenheim. Good evening."

Dora didn't know what she would do with it, either, for a while.

She fixed another drink. Even listening to Aldington made her nervous. Her facial muscles were stiff with obeying his unspoken command for total attention.

In a way, the story of the shot heard from Trunk Street was like the freshly turned earth in Aldington's garden. Something that, when she found it, she found she really hadn't wanted to.

But then she heard herself, casual, with an unspecified but amazed audience: "Aldy—you know the 'Good Morning with Aldington Show?'—actually he likes me to call him Kenneth—gave me a ring, and I followed the thing up. It was as simple as that. Heaven knows why he picked poor little me, that screams when she thinks she hears a mouse."

Seventeen

Well, she'd been wondering if there was some important break-through thing she could do tonight, hadn't she?

Before everything stopped, tomorrow. And boredom settled on her like dust.

Flo. Her mind landed on the name with a sudden jump. Flo Grattle, a friend from years back. Flo was a night owl, and a woman alone, too. No, not a woman alone; an independent woman free to do what she wanted, answerable to nobody. Like herself.

Flo lived in an apartment on Blenheim Court. That was why the name, after a second, had seemed familiar. Dora hadn't seen it. Flo had only moved in last month.

A goal, a safe warm destination. Go see Flo, and on the way, a block short of her house, just take a stroll, a look around. It wasn't really late, not even eleven.

Flo was at home. She said she had just washed her hair and couldn't go to bed for at least an hour. "Come on down, Dora, we'll have a housewarming. The place is a mess, but you'll understand."

"Goody," Dora said. Don't, she decided, tell Flo about Trunk Street and the shot. It was her secret. Aldington had especially wanted *her* to know. He obviously hadn't told anyone else. And it might be nothing, anyway. A blind alley.

That was funny. She giggled a little to herself as she finished her drink.

"Trunk Street is a blind alley," she murmured, and giggled again. She telephoned for a Yellow Cab.

By the time she had dressed and fixed her face, now patched with anxious red, and found a housewarming present for Flo—a nice little cactus in a pot shaped like an elephant which someone had given her for her last birthday; she hated cactus, but then lots of people didn't or there wouldn't be so much of it around—the taxi was blowing its horn in the street below.

For reassurance, she gave the driver Flo's address. When it came to the actual doing of it, she might not want to—

Dora Maunder, someone's admiring voice in her head said, wasn't a person given to hesitation and indecision—not that night, when there was so much at stake.

Her voice came out higher than she usually heard it. "Oh, I forgot —I want to get out at the corner of Trunk Street, driver."

Trunk Street. The words sounded dangerous in her mouth. Bodies in trunks.

The driver got out and came around and opened the door for her as she fumbled for bills and coins. Philadelphia taxi fares, she thought, were outrageous, although it was nice that they still sometimes opened the door for you. Catch a New York cab driver doing that.

The cab drove away and she was suddenly wrapped in absolute stillness. Trunk Street stretched before her, very narrow, very dark. There was a streetlight at the far end and a few lights in some of the houses. Were the darkened ones empty, or their occupants merely asleep?

There was a small grim warehouse on one corner at her end, a silent garage on the other. The houses began after that, small, old, some of them Father-Son-and-Holy-Ghost houses, one room to each of the three floors. She had memories of picking her way down treacherous curving pie-wedge stairs, without banisters or any kind of handhold, in such houses.

About halfway up the block, Aldington had said. All right, move, go halfway up Trunk Street. Her shoes sounded loud on the cracked pavement and she began to walk more softly. From somewhere up ahead came a faint thin tapping noise. Echoes of her own footsteps in the silent alley?

The house could be, then, number 214, or 216, or 218, on her left. Or possibly 215 or 217 across the way. From the center, left-hand house she heard the comforting murmur of a radio, coming from an upstairs back bedroom, to judge from the sound of it. ". . . cloudy and damp with possible thunderstorms late tomorrow."

She realized that she didn't know what she was looking for, exactly, but then she hadn't known what she was looking for when she peered into Aldington's garden or answered his phone call. She just sort of fell into things. Dora's luck, you might call it.

He wouldn't have lured her down here for anything . . . anything ghastly, would he? Hardly. After all, he was a public figure. With a reputation to maintain.

She began to shake inwardly. This was all terrifying. She wondered if it was really worth it after all. Flo's house was just a short block away. Flo and light and safety and talk and a drink.

". . . the dear souls are kindly paying me for two weeks vacation and gave me five hundred dollars as a down payment on my room in the old folks' home," her own bitter voice, to Millie, repeated to her.

She straightened her back. No matter what they said, she was a vigorous capable woman. There hadn't been anyone as efficient at Homans. Everybody knew it.

"In the strange case of Jonas Rath, it was Dora Maunder who singlehandedly . . ."

Another voice, preferably Gus Welcome's. "Can't let talents like yours go to waste, Dora. How would you like to come back as office manager, run your own show. . . . ?"

A truck went deafeningly by on Second Street, pouring a tide of its thunder into Trunk Street. Enough to wake the dead, Dora thought. The noise was worse than the silence; you couldn't hear if there was anything or anyone behind you. The noise died.

She forced herself to stay where she was, stand very still, listen. Well, there were her four or five houses, innocent-looking enough.

The house immediately to her right was a shabby brick, heavily curtained, with a high marble stoop and a driveway going back to a garage. On the far side of the driveway, just up ahead, was an empty burned-out shell of a house. Dangerous. Scandalous. It could topple at any time. Go on thinking how scandalous it is. Honestly, the way they run things in this city—

She took a step or two into the driveway, with a half-formed idea of seeing if Jonas's blue car was in the garage. Her eye was caught by something in a side window just above her head. An oblong of palish material, plywood probably, fitted into one of the windowpanes, looking wrong, looking evil, as though it might be covering . . . a hole made by a bullet. . . .

The steady sound she had thought might be the echo of her own footsteps thrown back at her—was that the pale oblong, being tapped into place in the window?

There was a footstep behind her. With a terrible lurch of the heart, she whipped her body around and said on a long astonished relieved breath, "Ohhhh . . . it's you."

Flo Grattle rumpled up the hair behind her ear. Still a bit damp, so that was all right; she'd have to stay up for a while, anyway. Dora must be having trouble getting a cab. It was almost forty-five minutes since she'd called. Of course, she had sounded a bit—but perfectly sensible, certainly good for a few more drinks. I can fix her up here, Flo thought, if it's too late or if she doesn't feel up to a cab home. She looked at the clock. A quarter to twelve.

At twelve, she called Dora's apartment. No answer. At twelve forty-five, puzzled, annoyed, and yawning, she set her hair and went to bed.

Eighteen

"Now, children, this dear little street, which is called Elfreth's Alley, dates from about 1700. Think of it, the little houses have been continuously in use for close to three hundred years."

Miss Viola Copio, with her group of twenty-three children in a straggling queue, gestured down the length of the illustrious alley. The fourth grade was having what the school called a History Walk. After studying this little street, they were to see Betsy Ross's cottage on Arch Street.

In the muffled sunlight, under a steamy sinister white sky, Elfreth's Alley looked as charming and gone and forgotten as a scene on a painted plate.

"See the old paving stones and look at all the different patterns of brick in the sidewalks," Miss Copio chanted. "Try to imagine the people these houses were originally built for, and the clothes they wore. Joann and William, don't stray ahead, stay with the class."

William, who was black and came from a region of awful poverty and unspeakable streets, had wandered with his small blond companion to gaze up in wonder at a window box burgeoning with petunias and geraniums and English daisies. Inside the wavery sparkling old glass panes of the window hung dazzling white ruffled organdy curtains. Curled up on the sill between the curtains, a white cat with one blue eye and one green one mewed soundlessly at him.

"These were the houses of river pilots, tailors, blacksmiths, cabinetmakers and pewterers," Miss Copio went on. "Do we all know what pewter is? Look, in the window of that blue house with the cream shutters. See the sort of gray dull-shiny little bowl? That's made of pewter."

The twentieth century rattled past in the air across the end of the street, which was only one block in length: the Frankford elevated train.

"Look to your left, in that courtyard, an old covered well. Isn't that a dear old well? People didn't have running water in those days. They had to get all their water from wells. Life wasn't as easy as we have it. There was no TV, no radio. Men and women had to work every minute."

"Did they have motorcycles then?" a ten-year-old asked in all innocence, gesturing at a dusty blue machine tilted into the angle of painted wooden cellar doors sloping into the sidewalk.

Miss Copio did not laugh, but said, "No, Laura. But that's a good example, class, of all the different generations of people who lived here, you might say from the age of the spinning wheel to the age of the motorcycle."

William and his friend Joann were still eight feet or so ahead of her. They were close to the end of the street, now. To their right was an empty weed-overgrown lot with a white fence around it.

"Stop at the corner," Miss Copio called. "There was a factory where that lot was. There was an awful fire and it burned down. A lot of these sweet old houses were in danger of burning down, too."

"Look," William said in a low voice. "There's a lady asleep."

"Where?"

"Under that big old piece of paper. See her arm?"

The weeds were thick and tall. Joann stared. Then she pulled her hand out of his and retreated to Miss Copio. The arm coming out from under the rain-soaked corrugated paper, which had once been a carton, had frightened her. A pale arm, palm up, with a gold bracelet around the wrist.

"Maybe she's drunk," William said sadly. "Look, Miss Copio. See her?"

Miss Copio did look, and uttered a small shriek before she could stop herself, and then said, "William, run back and tell Miss Magellan to take her group right over to Betsy Ross's cottage. Class, you follow him and join Miss Magellan. I have a little errand."

She shooed the children back up the street, where another section of the class could be seen entering. Then she knocked at the door of the house next to the empty lot and was admitted by a dumpy woman who listened in openmouthed horror as Miss Copio called the police and said:

"This may be a false alarm, and I don't want to give you needless trouble, but there may be a dead woman—I mean there is a woman who may be dead—lying under some paper in a vacant lot at the end of Elfreth's Alley. I'm a teacher and I have children with me. I couldn't—go in close enough to be sure—" And wouldn't, she added with a mental shudder.

Leaving the dumpy woman in a state of numbed astonishment, she ran out of the house and in a moment or so caught up with her group. The last straggler had just left the Second Street entrance to the alley when a siren screamed a block below.

Nineteen

The identification of the woman found strangled to death at the east end of Elfreth's Alley would certainly have taken a good deal longer than it did, if it hadn't been for a series of telephone calls.

No handbag was found. The woman wore a green and white checked cotton dress which showed, upon later examination, a John Wanamaker label, a pair of white sandals from the Tiptoe Shop on Chestnut Street, and a black nylon body stocking.

Usual thing, Sergeant Reilly thought, as he and Patrolman Pflautt waited for the homicide detective. Robbery and rape, the body left like a broken toy that isn't any fun to play with any more. Probably for ten, or fifteen, or twenty-five dollars in all. And maybe a credit card or two, and department store charge cards.

Flo Grattle was an early riser. She got up at six this morning as usual. She hadn't slept well. Off and on she had waked, worrying about Dora.

Last night she had dismissed Dora's nonappearance as a mild aberration: she had found something better to do, and forgotten to call, or she had had more to drink than Flo then gauged, and her intended visit had slipped her mind. But then the telephone—would she be so deeply asleep that she wouldn't hear it at all?

Flo guiltily considered the horrible things that happened every day and every night in Philadelphia, things you got so used to reading about in the newspapers and hearing about and seeing on radio and TV, the daily litanies of disaster, that your mind screened them out, finally, in a turning away that was part personal fear and part bleak boredom.

Too bad to wake Dora up if she was at home and asleep, but worse to wait, if she wasn't. At twenty minutes after six, she called Dora's apartment. There was no answer.

Ellen, roused at her shore cottage after a late night at a party, was confused, irritable, and just a little concerned.

"Perhaps she spent the night with someone. . . . I don't think she has a man—oh, dear, that sounds unkind—but at her age, she might have jumped into something silly. I'd hate to have the police hunting her and surprising her in her slip—"

She paused to think. "I know her landlady. I'll call her, have her look over the apartment and see if the bed's been slept in or if she's left a note, saying she was going to Longwood Gardens or New York or somewhere. After all she is on vacation. I'll call you back."

Families are great, Flo thought sourly. Who else could she call? That frightfully attractive next-door neighbor of Dora's. Jonas Rath.

Olivia answered, and upon being asked for Jonas, said, "Who is this who wants him and *why?*" in a voice weighted with suspicion.

Flo identified herself and said she was concerned about Dora and thought Jonas might know where she was.

"Talk about the pot asking the kettle," Olivia said, in a manner Flo found obscure. "I'll call my sister-in-law. She's friendly with Dora. Let me have your number in case I find anything out."

Ellen called Flo back. "The apartment's in order, the bed hasn't been slept in, her suitcases are all there. Let's let it go until noon or afternoon. It may be what I first thought it was . . ."

The telephone waked Millie from a terrifying dream of having lost Gus Welcome in the black cellars of an immense house and running, crying out his name, in the dark.

"Sorry to wake you," Olivia said. "A friend of the Maunder woman woke *me*. She was supposed to go to the friend's house last night and never turned up, it seems. I don't know what all the fuss is about. Women do occasionally abandon their own beds for more interesting ones, but I thought she might have been in touch with you—"

Fear struck with one tremendous thump of the heart.

Dora helping. Dora investigating. "Aldington's garden . . . there was a great long trough of freshly turned earth. . . ."

Shattner: "She's a troublemaker. She'd better watch out. . . ."

Dora, searching for Jonas's car. Put yourself in the hands of Detective Maunder.

"I think the police had better be called right away. I'll do it." A sense of being responsible settled on her shoulders, an intolerable load.

Rather than tackle the impersonal vastness of police headquarters, and sharply remembering Valiante's permissive view of missing persons, Millie found the number of the station house nearest Dora's apartment. They might even know Dora by sight.

As she was carefully describing Dora to the corporal in charge, ". . . about five feet three, in her early forties, short straight gray hair cut in bangs, pale blue eyes, a small mole or wen on the right cheekbone, capped front teeth, I think, and she'd be wearing a gold bracelet in a lily pattern . . . ," Millie had a rather hopeless, sinking feeling. She realized that the story of the unattached woman who had gone out at night and hadn't come back to sleep in her own bed was all too open to the obvious interpretation. Comfortably removed from danger. From death.

"Nothing's come in on anyone answering your description, at least so far," the corporal told her over an uncovered yawn. He asked for her name, address, and telephone number. She knew that she would be unable to bear the morning, the waiting, alone, and gave him Jonas's address and number. "If she doesn't turn up later," he said, "check back."

Oh my God, Millie thought, what if *she* disappears, too? Vanishes into Jonas's void. Another hole in the world. Forever.

Homicide Detective Salvatore Cane was the man assigned to the case of the Elfreth's Alley Body, as it was to be labeled by the local press.

The broken-doll woman, with her dreadful throat and eyes that, open in death, looked like a soundless scream of bloodshot blue, was examined and photographed and fingerprinted and removed in a police ambulance.

After having been kept at a tidy distance by the police, the residents of the tiny street and office workers and shopkeepers from the nearby business streets had nothing of more absorbing interest to watch than the uniformed men searching the weedy lot. The searchers found nothing for their pains but soft drink cans, two old tires, and an illegally dumped bag full of ancient garbage.

From the crush and bend of the weeds, from the position of the body, and the faint marks of the white flaking paint of the fence on the bare shins of the woman, it appeared that she had not been killed in the lot, but had been taken there, and half thrown, half dragged over the fence, and pulled fourteen and a half feet from it, into the tallest of the weed patches.

The paving stones of the alley would of course record no tire marks, if she had been brought there in a car, nor would the herringbone brick sidewalk yield up footprints.

The damp unfolded carton covering her had probably been meant to conceal her wholly, at least for a little while, but the arm must have escaped the murderer's notice.

After all, Cane said, he wouldn't want to use a flashlight to check and see if his girl was tucked up nicely, not with all those houses near. A preliminary examination on the spot placed the time of her death at somewhere between eleven and two in the morning; the night had been warm and without rain.

Cane, too, saw her as belonging to the sad legion of robbery and rape victims, until her probable identification, and the source of this identification, was radioed to him.

It took a tremendous effort to get past Gus's marble steps and fanlighted paneled white front door. Beyond that door lay the only safety and strength that had sustained her through these dislocated days. It was well after nine, anyway; he would probably have left for work. She sensed through brick and wood and shining glass that the house didn't hold him.

"Lord, Millie," Olivia said, "you look like Mrs. Doom. Relax, it's probably nothing. Even her sister says wait until noon or afternoon. I'll get you a cup of my own special reviving coffee."

From the kitchen, she called conversationally, "Can you believe he has less than four hundred dollars in his savings account? With his salary? There's a mutual fund thing, but of course it's taken a horrible beating. British Airways has been calling up wanting him to confirm a flight to London this Friday. Maybe he jumped the gun and went early—"

The telephone rang. Millie answered it shakily.

"Shattner here," the telephone said. "I tried to reach you at your hotel, and your answering service guided me onward and uptown." She had never heard him pleasant before, or trying to be. "Jim told me you've been worried about Jonas, and I thought you'd be relieved to hear he's finally deigned to position himself—"

She sat down very slowly and carefully on the arm of the sofa.

"—Key West somewhere—" the voice sending unreal echoes through her head, through the roaring in her ears. "Won't say where, says he has to have a marlin or two before he can return to active duty at Homans, the lazy bastard, but won't be gone for more than five or six days—"

"Then he's dead," Millie said, to herself, or to Shattner, she wasn't sure whom. What was that clicking noise? Oh. She had hung up on Shattner.

She was aware of Olivia's face, a foot or so away, eyes staring, huge. "Drink this," Olivia said, "and the sooner the better. Who's dead? Jonas again?"

She tried. Very hot strong coffee heavily laced with brandy. She politely excused herself, went into Jonas's bathroom and threw up, washed her face and mopped her eyes and came woodenly back into the living room.

"I've just been told Jonas is alive and well and in Key West and has to have a marlin or two," she said to Olivia, careful about each syllable. "You may or may not remember that Jonas couldn't bear to kill anything, except perhaps an occasional mosquito, and even that made him feel guilty. And he hates, loathes the tropics. We went once to Key West and when we left he said, 'For God's sake keep it and throw away the key. . . .'"

Olivia sighed heavily. "He could be anywhere, doing anything, this could just be dust in the eyes of the people who pay his salary. Delaying tactics. If only he weren't so damned *devious* in his ways. Make another try at the coffee, now that you've gotten rid of your breakfast."

There was a light sharp knock at the door. The man Olivia admitted was short and strongly built, with heavy shoulders, a square face with permanent troubled scowl lines between thick eyebrows over hooded dark eyes. He was in his late thirties. His shirt was white, his tie blue, his suit a darker blue.

"*Cane*," Olivia said to Millie quite loudly, as though trying to make a foreigner understand her language by raising her voice. "From the police, a homicide detective, finally—" and turning to him, hands on hips, she demanded, "And have you found him and is he alive or dead? This is beginning to be too much for me."

"Found him?" Salvatore Cane asked. "Found who?"

The big tall woman with the fussy blond wig looked as if she was waiting for a blow. The other woman, looking as if she had already had one, or several, drooped into a corner of the sofa, white, some kind of life gone out of her. But good-looking in spite of it all; fear and fatigue almost became her. Her doe eyes watched him, waiting for yet another wall to topple on her.

Make it quick. "You're Ms. Lester, who called the station house this morning about Dora Maunder? A dead woman was found in Elfreth's Alley this morning. She answers fairly exactly to the description you gave, including the mole on the right cheekbone, the capped teeth, and the fleur-de-lis bracelet."

Millie uttered a cry which sounded like the caw of a wounded bird.

Olivia said, "Christ! The poor thing. Can I get some coffee? I'll be right back."

"How was she killed?" Millie could hardly make her mouth work. It never occurred to her for an instant that Dora could have died a natural death.

"She was strangled and tossed into a vacant lot. Could have been carried there in a car. It happened around midnight or a little later. What's your relationship with her? Family? Friend?"

Corporal Hart, at the station house, had added to his report that the woman who had called in with the description sounded frantically worried.

"Neither," Millie said. "I only met her a few days ago. But I think it's because of me she's dead."

Olivia thrust a mug of coffee at him. Cane drank, coughed suddenly as the brandy hit his palate, stared at Olivia, and went on drinking without a change of expression.

Tears were running down Millie's face. She wiped them impatiently away.

"I'd better hear," Cane said, "why you think she's dead because of you."

He listened impassively to her story. It was concise and intelligent, in spite of shock and sadness. ". . . I'm beginning to think," she said, coming to the end of it, "that whatever's happened to him had something to do with his office, his work—"

She named no names. Vague but strengthening convictions was one thing; offering murder suspects to the police was another.

". . . she was very much alone. There wasn't any excitement in her life, I think. She was desperately eager to be involved . . . and then she adored Jonas, he had been kind to her. I'm afraid she went to perhaps ridiculous lengths to try and find a trace of him. . . ."

Why, he thought, was she pushing it so hard?

She got his unspoken message clearly. Who needs fancy explanations for a crime like this? A woman alone, wandering about at night in a dangerous part of town, robbed and then casually, brutally extinguished.

So what else is new?

And here she was, with her bizarre story, trying to muddle up a perfectly clear and ordinary case, present intricate mysteries to a badly overworked police force.

Cane got up from his chair. He said, "If there should possibly—I mean, if something turns up in the next day or so that connects her with your husband, it would be helpful if you'd stay around." His tone implied, There's just the one chance in a hundred we might need you. "You're perfectly free to go back to New York if you want, but—"

"No. I'll stay."

Cane, who found himself attracted to her, said with a half-smile from the doorway, "And just in case—while *you're* hunting your husband—don't make any appointments in dark alleys with people you don't know."

As the door closed behind him, she looked down and found her fingers flickering over the telephone like uncertain butterflies.

Gus. She had to. No.

She fought it for four minutes and then dialed Homans.

Robin said, "Oh, he's in New York today, videotaping a Fairacres Peaches commercial for Friendship, and then he was invited to an awards dinner tomorrow night in California"—her voice warmed with pride—"for a commercial he did for Guardian. He didn't just get *a* medal, he got *the* medal. He was in two minds about going, but I made a reservation anyway on the nine o'clock to Los Angeles. One of his sisters lives out there, so he can pay a family visit, too. Any message in case he calls in?"

The telephone in her hotel room had rung while she was in the shower. Her toweled and dripping dash had been too late. Now she wondered if it had been Gus.

I have to go to New York, will you share a seat on the train with me before we go our separate ways?

"No. No message."

Ellen and Joe McGuire drove up from the shore in the afternoon, went whitely to the city morgue, and formally identified Dora. Ellen wept with a guilty kind of grief.

Joe said, "I hope it doesn't come out in the papers that she was mixed up in something queer, drugs or something. You don't know these days."

Ellen, blotting tears, angry that guilt should be mixed in with shock and sorrow, said:

"Oh, Joe. This is going to spoil the whole summer."

Twenty

Cane went next to Dora Maunder's apartment. There was just the off chance that she had been killed there and the body taken to Elfreth's Alley to delay discovery, identification.

The place was neat, clean, bright. No disorder of any kind. A clean plate and glass and knife and fork on the drainboard. Her typewriter, set close to the living room window, had a sheet of yellow paper on which she had apparently been typing some of her detecting notes. He scanned it quickly and automatically.

"Jonas's car. Could it just plain have been stolen and its missing be only a coincidence? Two cars stolen within three blocks here last week. Remind Millie to report it as stolen to the police and then they'd have to try to trace it? Illegal, maybe."

Cane grinned. He made a note to himself to have a three-state alert put out for Jonas Rath's car. It wouldn't hurt.

In a crazy way, there could be a connection. Thin, remote, but it had occurred to him, next door, that it was funny that Millicent Lester had gotten a telephone call about her husband's turning up in Key West right on the heels of Dora's murder, just when the two separate cases might have been expected to touch edges in that distressed young woman's mind. A call meant to reassure, shut her up, send her back to New York, dismiss for a week at least any more wondering about Rath. And a week was a lot of time for someone to make other arrangements about his life or his whereabouts.

He returned to the typed notes. Probably meaningless. Millie had told him about Dora's having lost her job of eighteen years at

Homans, and these notes sounded backbiting, the kind of muttering you'd hear in any office, anywhere—

"Does S's wife know, about him, and just put a good face on things? Or doesn't she know at all? Jonas does, and I don't think he's wrong about things like that. He's been around.

"Ryan's boys. Is he all that crazy about them, boring you to death with bloody baseball and football and Little League and forward passes, or is it an act to cover up running after les girls, make him sound like a devoted family man?"

He looked with real interest at the last typed notation.

"Now, ten forty-five, call from Aldington, Kenneth, that is. Quite nice and friendly, after that horrible business the other night. Might be something in it. Especially now, with Millie going home tomorrow. No time, damn it."

No time indeed.

Cane approached Aldington with care and courtesy.

Although he wasn't the Liberty Bell or Betsy Ross's cottage or the slab marking the grave where Benjamin Franklin was not buried, and on which people threw pennies, he was a Philadelphia celebrity who was now beginning to assert not only regional but national interest.

He was taping the second of two shows, his secretary said; after which his custom was to go directly home for tea and a nap.

Could he spare Homicide Detective Cane a few minutes? After a ridiculously long wait on the phone, she returned and said, yes, a very few minutes. Would the police be obliging enough to call at his private residence at twelve forty-five?

"Poor soul," Aldington said. Yes, he had heard about Dora on the noon news, and scanned the newspaper on his way home in the taxi. "We live with violence, do we not? Of course, this—annihilation—must be a cliché in your working day."

His attitude annoyed Cane, perhaps because it came so flatfootedly close to his own views.

They were sitting in the living room. Aldington was sipping tea from a flowered china cup and nibbling a thin cucumber sandwich.

"I believe Dora Maunder had some kind of encounter with you several evenings ago?"

"Yes, poor wench," Aldington said. "She came sniffing and all but trespassing over my garden wall with some mindless tale about a lost cat. My gardening chap had been spading earth for some young weeping willows I'm transplanting from my house in the country and she quite bridled at the sight of the fresh soil."

"Why was she so interested in your gardening?"

"She's hunting like a demented bloodhound for a man named Jonas Rath, who seems to be mislaid somewhere. Interesting word for what he may have been up to. He has an irresponsible way of disappearing and amusing himself on his rather outrageous consulting salary. One gathers he is now murdering marlin somewhere in Florida."

He got out a pipe and became busy with it. "As for Dora, she may have had a grave in mind."

"And the telephone call before eleven last night? You may have been the last person who talked to her alive."

Aldington took a puff and savored it. "The call, yes—heavens, was it that late? I wanted her to do some typing on six pilot columns I've been invited to write, to be nationally syndicated—'Aldington's U.S.A.' I'd heard that she did this sort of thing on the side and quite cheaply, too."

He poured another cup of tea. "You'll pardon me if I say I don't understand all this conscientious poking and prying. One naturally assumes it's the usual thing: woman out on her own in the dark of night . . . the rape, the robbery, or perhaps the other way around, and then the real fun, the killing. At least that's how one thinks these people feel when they're getting their kicks. Revenge on the whites, and so on."

What he was really doing, Cane thought, was asking for hard information: how much they really knew, so far, about the circumstances of Dora Maunder's death.

"Furthermore, I'm as a matter of fact consumed with curiosity to know how you came to be informed of my telephone call. If the newspaper accounts are correct, she must have left her house almost immediately after I called and never did get where she was going, to her girl chum's apartment."

"She was keeping a sort of logbook of notes on people she suspected, in connection with Rath. For some reason she added your call to her collection. Have you any idea why? Considering it was an ordinary business matter, typing."

Aldington shrugged. "It was a call from *me*, the first she'd ever gotten, and oh dear, the last. Perhaps she thought it was an event in itself worth noting down. Or, more practically, to remind herself of the assignment. These ladies who live alone and sip vodka tend to get scatty and forgetful about what happened the night before."

Cane got up to go. "How was her manner when you talked to her?"

"Perfectly normal, I should imagine, for her. A bit gushy and silly."

"And she was going to undertake the work you wanted her to do?"

Aldington looked him straight in the eye and smiled.

"Of course."

Cane took away two puzzling impressions from his interview. Probably, he thought, of no importance anyway—

One, that Aldington was lying about the phone call. Otherwise, why take the trouble, and the slight risk, to ask how the police knew about it?

And two—this feeling vague, unformulated—that his final "Of course" had some unpleasant glee behind it, a sense of some secret almost too big and amusing to contain.

The interview with the bereaved family: routine but always, after no matter how many times, unwillingly faced.

"I won't detain you long, Mrs. McGuire, Mr. McGuire."

The McGuires had gone back to the Spruce Street apartment to meet Cane. Ellen was red-eyed, drinking cup after cup of black coffee. Joe McGuire had bought a bottle of scotch on the way in and was gloomily sipping at a hefty dark double or triple on ice.

Did they know of anything in Dora's private life which could lead to her murder?

No, nothing.

"She was the unlucky one," Ellen said, as though she had to tell someone. "She had the care of our mother when girls of her age were running around getting themselves married. Dora was quite pretty in her twenties and early thirties. In these last years, I'm afraid she's

been lonely, and the job loss was a frightful shock to her, and sham-
ing, too."

"She was a good cook," Joe said unexpectedly, looked surprised at
himself, flushed, and retreated to his drink.

"This Jonas Rath thing seemed to have given her a new lease on
life," Ellen went on. "Sort of like a treasure hunt. She was excited and
happy about helping out."

"There wasn't a man?"

"That ended months ago. He was married."

"It couldn't have started up again? And she put pressure on him,
threatened to tell his wife, something like that?"

"No. I always got an hour-by-hour description of her troubles with
Chris. . . ."

"But—someone you wouldn't know about?"

"Not a chance. She'd always boast like mad about even the most
casual date or a party or anything, so we'd think she was having a
great social life."

Ellen burst into tears. Her sobbing was ripped through with hysterical laughter.

"Wouldn't it be funny if Jonas turned up alive and Dora died for
nothing? I mean, the two things may have nothing at all to do with
each other. It may be just what everybody seems to think—but
wouldn't it be screamingly *funny* . . . ?"

Twenty-one

"I can't find the checkbook for his regular checking account. Surely he doesn't carry it around with him, not with credit cards? Perhaps he keeps it at his office—"

Faced with a choice between Olivia's practical monetary speculations—which could be her own defense against a ghost, creeping ever closer—and immediate work, however unreal, she chose work.

She told Olivia she had a drawing waiting for her at Homans and would Olivia mind if she went and got on with it?

Olivia said, "I suppose it's perfectly safe in broad daylight. People don't do things to people in offices, do they?"

People, Millie said to herself, do awful things to other people in offices, but actual manslaughter or murder was rare.

She walked through gray sticky heat to the tall building on Walnut Street. It was between twelve and one and like other advertising agencies at lunchtime Homans wore the air of an abandoned city.

A plump girl at the switchboard, relieving the pink-blonde, swore under her breath at her board. Inside, telephones rang despairingly. Going into her cubicle, she saw Shattner rush from his office to take a call at his secretary's desk, heard him say, "Handbag *what*? Handbag repair—Wanamaker's—?" choking with annoyance. She started to laugh to herself and then caught it back. The laughter didn't feel right, and there was no way of knowing where it would stop.

Across the hall and down a door, Gus's office was unlit and profoundly empty. His telephone started ringing. Shattner, having hung up loudly on Wanamaker's, took a step toward his door, said,

"Jesus Christ, this is too much—" and saw Millie, quietly seating herself at her drawing board.

He came in and closed the cubicle door behind him. The room was small, about ten by ten feet, and it contracted almost visibly. He was breathing hard, perhaps with rage at the telephones.

"You're an abrupt young woman, aren't you," he said in a soft ugly voice. "I thought I was doing you a favor. Telling you about hearing from Jonas. My reward is a sharp crash in the ear."

He picked up her metal T square and fingered it in his heavy hands. Nerves, maybe; his eyes were tired and bloodshot and looked everywhere but directly into hers.

Millie got up from the board. "I suffer mildly from claustrophobia, particularly in windowless rooms," she said. She opened the door wide. "Was it you who Jonas called?"

"No, he didn't have the guts to talk to me. He called his secretary —she's on vacation, down at the shore somewhere—and had her call here with the message."

"Do you have her number?"

"No," Shattner said, "and I have no idea where she's staying. Since you sicked the police on us the other day, I thought I'd let them know, too. They thanked me nicely, but I must say they didn't show any burning interest in the little matter of Jonas Rath."

"Well, Amos," a woman said, in the doorway. She was tall, taller than he, and severely handsome, without makeup, her skin scoured and shining with health. She studied Millie with open rudeness.

"Alma—" Shattner moved away from his position close beside the board. "A nice surprise—let's go into my office—"

"And you couldn't," she said crisply, "manage half an hour to take me to lunch. I didn't know overseeing the—artwork around here was one of your heavy responsibilities. Or was I interrupting mere socializing?"

His face went a dark red. "I left my office to catch the telephone— the goddamn place is deserted. I'm going to have a short talk with the office manager—"

"How vice-presidential of you . . . darling," Alma Shattner said, "taking calls for clerks. I'm due at the dentist in twenty minutes.

If you can spare a little of your working time, you might just tear yourself away and repair with me to your office."

It should have been refreshing to see the bully bullied in his turn, but it wasn't. Millie found herself unable to look at Shattner's face.

He followed his wife abjectly out of the cubicle. She heard Alma Shattner say, "I've had this letter, note rather, from Jonas." Each word was like the jab of an icepick. "About you."

His office door closed.

Millie put her head in her hands.

He could have given a note to someone. Mail this if I don't show up after a few days—

Work. Don't think, work. She was reminded suddenly of her early childhood, wanting to be told, every other minute, when they were going to the beach today. During those summers, it was the most important destination in the world. And her mother would look up from her book and say, "Presently, Millie, presently."

Presently, Jonas would disappear forever.

Or presently, Jonas would explain himself or be explained.

Presently, life would collect itself again around a firm sane center.

But would Dora's ghost, drifting by on her left, always haunt her, while Jonas's strode along on her right?

No. It was unfaceable. It would all be clarified and painfully, finally dismissed. Presently.

She dashed in the watercolor calico costume on her pencil drawing, mixed soft dark gray and ginger and white for the calico cat on her girl's lap, flicked in the cat with her brush, and then concentrated hard on the girl's face and kerchiefed head. She would give Gus a fairly comprehensive rough and then, later, in some unimaginable peace in her apartment in New York—if he okayed her rough—she would do the finished drawing. With Eleventh Street and its trees, her own world, looking reassuringly into her window. With Mike Garland coming around later to take her out to dinner.

Mike Garland? What did he look like? Gus's features superimposed themselves ruthlessly on the other man's, obliterated Mike Garland's pleasant long-jawed eager face.

A girl who looked like a slightly less expensive version of Amanda

Graves—long blond hair, huge pale blue sunglasses, pearled skin and lips—put her head in at the door.

"Mr. Ryan wonders if you would mind coming in to see him with your Calico Cat stuff."

Millie, well used to office elbowing and one-upping and asserting of authority, said, "Yes, tell him to give me ten minutes or so."

Ryan's office was large and self-consciously male, burly tweed upholstery, whiskey-colored rug, cruel elephant's-foot wastebasket, an antique rifle on mounts on the wall, large studio portraits of what must be his wife and sons standing in leather frames on top of long low shelves.

He got up to greet her and then sat down again and put his feet up on his desk, squarely in her face.

"The sketch is wet. Please lay it flat," Millie said. "Though it will be hard for you to look at it with your feet where they are."

"You sound like Gus Welcome," Ryan said, and then added, "but soft and sweet, a regular thrush. He'd never be able to utter like that." He put his feet under his desk. "I'm not interfering, mind, but I have to keep on top of things. You artists—*all* you artists—are delightfully impractical, and somebody's got to ride herd."

Practicing being president, Millie thought. Flexing his muscles at her.

He studied the drawing. "I'd say you were close," he said. "Not quite there, girl, but close. . . ."

"I don't know anything about art, but I know what I like," Millie said recklessly. To hell with Calico Cat if Ryan was going to ride herd on it.

He looked up sharply. "Don't be taking offense like that . . . just offering an opinion . . . my measuring rod is, would Goosey like it? My wife, Goosey. Gertrude. Mrs. Consumer, I call her. Great gal, by the way. Too bad you won't be here long enough to meet her. Gus said you were heading back for New York—"

"In a few days."

"Oh—changed your mind? Or—waiting for lazybones to get back from the Keys?"

For some reason she chose not to tell him the police had requested her to stay.

"Yes, waiting for lazybones," she said. "Waiting for Jonas."

She wondered if his herd-riding and clumsy art criticism had been, after all, just a device to find out if Jonas's supposed call had achieved its objective and sent her homeward.

(Olivia: "I suppose it's perfectly safe . . . people don't do things to people in offices . . .")

She got up from her chair and picked up her drawing. "I'll let Gus decide exactly how close this is to what he asked for, and then you two can thrash it out between yourselves."

"I don't like the word thrash. The fella's bigger than I am," Ryan said, all jollity again. "Keep in touch, Jonas's Millie. One of my weaknesses is liking to know what pretty girls like you are up to."

She had to pass the closed door of Shattner's office to reach her cubicle. From behind it came the muffled, wrenching, unmistakable sound of a man trying not to be heard, face buried in something, weeping.

Twenty-two

To escape the sound, or leave it to its own privacy, she closed the door of her little borrowed room and went to clean up the working table beside her board.

The door was flung open and she turned, frightened, and was immediately in Gus's arms.

"Oh my God, Millie . . ." cherishing fingers moving through her hair, protecting body tight and strong against hers. He sounded winded, as though he had been running hard.

He let her go after what couldn't have been more than a few seconds, and reclosed the door.

"I thought at first you were in New York—"

"I thought you'd soon be heading for Los Angeles—"

"Robin called me about Dora. I tried to get you at your apartment, and then I thought you might be on the train. Your answering service said you were still here, which I couldn't believe, but—"

"How on earth did you get back so fast? Robin said you were videotaping. . . ."

"There's a plane that takes off from the river at Twenty-second Street and lands at a pier below Society Hill Towers. Does it in half an hour. I got Olivia when we landed—she'd been out before—and she told me the police had asked you to stay—"

"I thought it was the least I could do for Dora."

Carefully and quietly, he opened the door behind him, and stood listening. Typing noises, laughter from somewhere. The sobbing sounds had ceased. From somewhere up the corridor:

Ryan: ". . . we'll go into the conference room and run through some kines to see which ones we want for summer repeats while you're on vacation. . . ."

Aldington: "I have some thoughts on that. I've already winnowed them down, mentally. . . ."

The voices were coming closer.

Gus said crisply to Millie, "Sara, you remember my sister Sara, is looking forward to seeing you. I told her you'd given up your hotel room and were moving into your usual corner room on Delancey Street where, if you'll excuse the expression, you'll be very welcome—"

Footsteps, muffled on the thick broadloom, reached the open door. Ryan looked in and said, "Hi, fella—" and, over his shoulder, to Aldington, "Gets a commercial in the can in ten minutes flat with his eyes shut. We didn't expect you back for days, Gus. You don't seem to have the normal instinct for stretching out a job, sleeping late, playing around, or with luck my boy, combining both. . . ."

"Three hours took care of Fairacres Peaches," Gus said. "My family's descending on me. I took a plane back. But I'm not available for any problems you might have. I only came in here to collect Millie."

"A happy chore. Get on with it, and see you tomorrow," Ryan said, grinning amiably. A moment later Millie heard him say, "What's this?—Amos's door is locked, and he told me he wanted to sit in on our meeting. I'll give him a call from the conference room. If it was anyone else, I'd think it was a post-martini nap, but Mrs. Amos doesn't approve of midday drinking."

"Thank you for verbally moving me into your house," Millie said, smiled, and added, "under your eaves."

"Not verbally. Physically. We are going now to your hotel and pick up your belongings, and then we will proceed homeward."

"Gus, no, this is ridiculous—"

"—If I have to carry you," he said, looking as if he thoroughly meant it. "You more or less handed yourself into my safekeeping, you know. For the moment you're my responsibility."

She looked silently at him, hesitating.

"—You can practice virtue and loyalty there just as well as you've done on your own," Gus said. "But until you're safely out of this town, this is how we're going to do it. I should never have let you have the key. I should never have let you come here. I told you there was something wrong, bad, about Jonas's job—but I looked the other way because business intrigues bore the hell out of me."

"Stop accusing yourself," Millie said. "I would have come here no matter how hard you put your foot down. And I'm tired and still not thinking right and Dora's . . . death hasn't hit bottom yet. I haven't quite believed it yet. . . . Does this mean you're taking my fantasies seriously? About Jonas?"

"I've taken everything about you seriously since you got off the escalator at Thirtieth Street. —Yes. I think you might be in horrible danger—no other word for it. If poor Dora stumbled onto something —and I don't buy the convenient rape, robbery, and murder theory —and was killed for it—"

"I think she was," Millie said steadily. "In some strange way, I know she was."

"So do I," Gus said. "And she's just, or was just, on the fringe. You're at the center. How can anyone know what Jonas told you? He wasn't noted for his discretion."

Past tense, now, no question in his voice.

She felt chilled and sad. "Thank you, I will gladly take the corner room on Delancey Street. Will your sister really be there?"

"No. She's in Paris. And there are three of them. Sisters, I mean. Sara and Louise and Ursula. But, Millie"—he smiled at her, his shoulders dropped, and he suddenly looked very tired—"you're the last woman in the world, I'd say, to need a chaperone."

There was a picture of Dora in the late afternoon edition of the *Bulletin,* along with an expanded and freshened-up report on her murder. Ellen McGuire had supplied the photograph, a snapshot of Dora taken three years ago at the shore cottage. Sitting in the sun on the beach with her arms hugging her knees, smiling at the camera, looking young and almost pretty. Good figure in a white bathing suit. In black and white, her gray Dutch bob looked fetchingly blond. All this made her death more interesting to the *Bulletin's* readers, more ladylike, dramatic, unsordid.

A taxi driver saw the photograph and got in touch with police headquarters and said he was sure that this was the woman, the fare, he had driven the night before from Cypress Street to Trunk Street.

He thought it was a bit strange at the time, he said, because Trunk looked like a nowhere street, more an alley, like, and she seemed frightened and not knowing exactly where she was going.

Trunk Street. A third of a block from Blenheim Court, where Flo Grattle had been expecting her.

Flo Grattle, when Cane called her, was puzzled. "I have no idea why she'd get out there instead of driving right up to my door. Unless she confused the two streets, forgot the name of mine. She hadn't been there yet—I only moved in a short while back. Or she could have wanted some fresh air, a little walk before she had another drink. Although at that hour, in this town . . ."

Cane called Ellen McGuire. Did she know if her sister knew anyone on Trunk Street?

"No—I don't know, she could have. It's a new name to me."

The residents of Trunk Street had neither seen nor heard anything of Dora Maunder, the Elfreth's Alley Body, at any time after 11 o'clock the night before. One old woman, bed-bound, who lived with an elderly daughter, said she'd heard a car door slam at the end of the street around eleven-thirty. But she wasn't sure. The trucks going by on Second Street made such a terrible racket, you couldn't get a wink's sleep some nights. It was a shame, the city should do something about it, when people couldn't sleep in their beds for the noise of trucks—

"There, Mother, the policeman doesn't want to hear about your insomnia," her daughter said.

Amanda Graves met Aldington at the Barclay Bar at six. She knew he would be terrified that she would turn up in jeans, and it amused her on this occasion to look like a proper rich girl: slender white silk dress, pearls, her shining hair tied back with a white chiffon scarf that floated to her waist. People looked at her. Aldington gave her his best smile, not the lip-lifted one baring his well-cared-for teeth.

"Well, Aldy?" She sipped her gimlet. "How are you coming with your assignment? Finding our boy, I mean."

"Let's say I've set the machinery in motion."

"By the way, that woman in the newspapers, Dora Something.

Didn't she used to be at Homans? You must have known her to talk to—"

"Dora Something. Rather a sad obituary but perhaps suitable." He lifted his glass and frowned at it. "Waiter, are you *quite* sure this is J and B?"

Twenty-three

With a gnawing feeling of wasting his time, Homicide Detective Cane visited Homans, Incorporated.

The switchboard-receptionist was informative.

"Dora—God, I cried all through my lunch hour"—she brushed away a tear—"worked for Ryan, but it was Shattner who fired her. He does things like that for Ryan. Ryan has a very soft Irish heart, he likes to think."

She said gleefully into her speaker, "Police to see you, Mr. Shattner."

Cane heard the snarled answer, "Tell him to wait. I have someone in my office. I'll call you back when I'm ready."

"I'd say fifteen minutes," the girl said. "There's probably no one in there at all. With him it's always wait fifteen minutes. For everybody."

Cane shuffled magazines; he had already read *Newsweek* and *Time* and found he could not interest himself in *Vogue*. Thank God for *National Geographic*.

When the door was grudgingly opened to him, after sixteen minutes, Cane was smooth and amiable. Routine inquiries—won't take up much of your time. Did Mr. Shattner know anything which might shed any light on Dora's murder? Any office troubles or conflicts?

He was interested in and embarrassed by the fact that Shattner had obviously been crying, unless he had awful sinus trouble or something. Grief for Dora, whom he had fired?

Shattner looked at him and through him and Cane had an eerie feeling that for this red-eyed man he didn't exist at all.

After a pause, Shattner said, "Conflicts? No. She was just a secretary, you know." His voice was raw and still wet. "Very efficient while she was on the job. But selfish about working time-clock hours. Wasn't interested enough in challenges to pitch in and stay late and give up a weekend here and there. We had to get someone younger. More dedicated."

"Had she any close friends here who might know more about her than you do?"

"I have no idea. I didn't follow her office social life. Perhaps one of the girls— But our staff has been ridiculously disorganized all day, just because— No, I can't have the office tied up any further."

Cane was by no means a softhearted man, but he didn't like to hear Dora Maunder's mortal remains dismissed like a swatted fly.

"I suppose you're a close associate of Jonas Rath," he said. Careless, blind shot. Direct hit.

Raging red surged up over the collar of Shattner's plum and lemon striped shirt.

"What the bloody hell is this? I thought you were here to ask about Maunder? What the hell has Jonas to do with it?"

"Now, now," from the hall. "Raised voices. Language."

A tall red-haired man, hands in his pockets, lounged into the office. As Shattner was mute, Cane and Ryan exchanged introductions.

"For God's sake, the man's only doing his duty," Ryan said. After one look, he carefully averted his eyes from Shattner's face as from some indecency. "I heard you mention Jonas. We have some interest in that matter, too, although I suppose police business doesn't include chasing down a deep-sea fisherman absent without official leave. . . . About Dora, how soon will they, uh, release the body so that we can send the appropriate? She worked here eighteen years, God bless her and rest her—"

"Tomorrow. And about Rath, it seems Dora was very interested in finding out where he is."

Ryan grinned. "Naturally. Jonas is somewhat of a stallion. She adores the fella, must miss having him next door. If you want to know all about Dora's secret heart, you might like to talk to Genevieve Coe, our receptionist. She and Dora palled around. I'll see that she's relieved immediately."

Genevieve Coe had no helpful information about Dora. Only more tears. "Those bastards—sorry, you didn't hear me. But it was such a lousy rotten thing to do to her—and to think I had a vodka and tonic with her just a few days ago—"

And then, the words coming out convulsively, like a hiccup: —"except, officer—" as though she was speaking aloud the second half of a sentence already begun in her head.

"Except what?"

Maddeningly, she said, "I guess officer is the wrong title, you're a big shot. Pardon."

"Was there something else about Dora that you were about to say?"

"No, nothing else about *Dora* . . . and I forget what else I was going to say. I guess I'm just upset."

Later, she discussed it with her current man, over sweet Manhattans and thick rare steaks.

"Dora kept calling and calling, wanting to know if Jonas Rath had checked in. She sounded mysterious, like Mata Hari or something. She wouldn't say why she wanted him but said it was terribly important. I almost told the police about it, but, I mean, why get involved? Don't you agree? D'you think I did the right thing?"

The man, who was interested in filling her up to the point where she would ask him back to her apartment for a nightcap, said, yes, why get involved?

Nevertheless, it niggled at her, although without in any way spoiling the steak and after it the vanilla ice cream half drowned in chocolate syrup and chopped pecans.

Last night she thought she had seen Jonas Rath. She had just managed to make her five-fifteen bus. She pushed up the stairs and clutched at a handhold on the corner of one of the seats. The sudden surge of the bus flung her toward the window, and she saw the tall figure with the golden lion locks turn in to the coffee and sandwich shop on the opposite corner of Market Street.

Funny. Hadn't someone said he was in Florida?

"I had a standing order from Shattner to nail him, hold him on the line, if he called in. Not that I would've, I'm on his side. He's a doll, madly good-looking—well, no, not more than you, but you're dark, that really gets to me— Anyway, after the bus driver missed out on dumping me on the floor, a truck stopped dead in front of us and I had time to really look. He was standing up at the counter, facing the window, drinking a cup of coffee. He had on a raincoat, a caped kind of one, and I thought it was a bit warm for that, but of course they did say on the weather that there was a sixty percent chance of rain, and he had on his dark glasses, wraparound ones. I thought, If that's not Jonas Rath I'm not Genevieve Coe. And then the bus started again and something about the way he put down his cup made me think I was wrong, although I couldn't be. . . ."

"Forget it, it's none of your business," the man said jealously, not liking her absorption in her subject. "To hell with the office, we're out for fun. Have another Manhattan."

"After *dinner?*"

"Why not?"

"You're a sport. Okay. Why not?"

And—being deeply preoccupied as she was by the man, and the Phillies having gotten off to such a bad start, and the chance of her winning maybe fifty thousand dollars in the New Jersey lottery, she successfully forgot that maybe she had seen Jonas Rath drinking coffee in Dewey's on Market Street.

Softly and quietly, but not irreverently, Gus said to himself, "Jesus Christ."

He was at the top of the wide stairway at the side of his house, outside Jonas's door. There was a brown cafe curtain on the window, with the upper half clear, looking out into the grapevines and ivy.

He glanced at his watch, waited two full minutes, and then pressed the doorbell.

Olivia, creamily blond and curled again, female again, in a businesslike navy blue robe, peered out of the window and opened the door.

She looked and sounded lonely. "Oh, come in—your own premises after all. Anything about Jonas—?"

"No, but I'd like to come in anyway."

He had left Millie unpacking her bag in the corner bedroom and domestically wanting to know where the ironing board and iron were, if he had such things in his possession. In the midst of death and danger, she said mournfully, "I have only these two *things*. . . ." and he told her Sara kept a closetful of clothes in the room next door. "She likes to stay here two or three months out of the year. She's not married yet, or at least not on paper, witnessed . . . and she's about your size. Help yourself."

"Can I get you a drink?" Olivia asked. "I was just beginning to be thirsty."

"Yes. I'll get it. Martini for you, too?"

"Yes, please."

Still a little unnerved, he found himself saying politely as he stirred ice cubes, "Are you comfortable here? Is there anything you need?"

"As comfortable as anyone can be who doesn't know from minute to minute whether their brother is alive or dead," Olivia said rebukingly. "I all but have a heart attack every time the phone rings." She sighed and added, "He's always loved playing games, keeping other people off balance. I think when people grow up they should stop teasing people. . . ."

Gus took a restoring swallow of his drink. "I have a favor to ask. Will you come downstairs and spend a few hours with Millie? I have to go out, and I don't want her alone. She's in a bad state, after Dora—"

"Happy to. I'm in a bad state myself," Olivia said, "although let's face it, Dora's in a worse one. . . ."

She studied Gus with a certain detachment and pleasure. "I must say Millie is lucky to have you to take care of her. Some people always have to go it alone— Wait, I'll dress and we can go down now if you want. I'd love to escape this trap for a while."

They found Millie trying, in the living room, to read a newspaper. She had put on a water-green linen dress of Sara's, but she looked as if something had blown out all the incandescent color in her skin and eyes and hair.

"Millie, the broken record again," she said flatly. "I stumbled on your cousin Farnall on the society page. With his wife. You may be interested to hear they entertained four hundred people last night. Anyway, something I had mentally lost just came back. Just before, on the phone, the shooting sound happened, Jonas changed the whole pitch of his voice and called me Mr. Farnall and said, 'Let's get down to business.' And that he didn't want to trouble me, but when I heard what he had to say—and then it happened."

"Millie, *dear*," Olivia said in a concerned way. "Just coming across people's names in papers—"

Gus said, "Pick up the phone there. I'll go into the kitchen and call him."

A minute later, his voice, strong, urgent. "Evening, Brace, get me Mr. Farnall, please . . . Augustus? Do you know or have you ever talked to a Jonas Rath?"

There was a considering silence. "Not that I know of, Gus." Leisurely tone, mashed-potato Main Line accent. "Should I?"

"I have a few more names for you. Stop and think if any one of them is familiar to you. James Ryan. Amos Shattner. Kenneth Aldington."

Another silence. "The Aldington fellow, yes, seen his program. Never met him personally, can't imagine I want to. Rather a cold wind out of the east, I'd say. But the other two men . . . it wouldn't be Cornelius Ryan you were thinking of?"

"No. This one's an advertising man."

"An *advertising* man!" Augustus Farnall said in innocent astonishment. "You're the only advertising man I know, Gus. Sorry I can't be more helpful. Say hello to Janey."

"Can't now, I'm in a great hurry. Give her my love."

He went back into the living room. He found Millie with her head buried in her hands. "Nowhere," she was saying. "Nowhere, nowhere . . ." her voice rising dangerously.

He pulled her to her feet, hard. "Stop it, Millie. If you've ever needed your wits about you, it's now."

She made the classic response of the female when ordered back from the luxury of hysteria to discipline and sanity:

"You're hurting me."

"Sorry." He gave Olivia, watching avidly, a nervous glance and then very gently kissed Millie on the cheek.

A cherishing sort of man. Perhaps it was all those sisters, perhaps he'd known what women were like from infancy, accepted it, forgave it, embraced it.

"Gus, I would like a drink," she said, voice warm and owning itself again. "After that it's my turn to cook your dinner."

"Thanks, but I have to go out—not for long. Cook dinner anyhow, don't wait for me. The last time I looked there were chops and things."

While he was pouring her scotch, the knocker sounded. He admitted a very large, very fat man with a tool kit.

Gus introduced them. "Arne Jonsen. Carpenter, gardener, plumber, majordomo. Without him I couldn't be a house dweller, much less a landlord. There's a wobble in one of the legs of the dining-room table, Arne, and a pane of glass has come loose in the china cabinet."

Millie understood quite clearly that the large fat man was there to watch over them while Gus was out.

"Where are you going?" Fear almost closed her throat.

He went to get his trenchcoat from the hall closet and came back with it.

"Rain's started again. . . . I have a private life, remember? You only walked into it four days ago." The voice light and cool, choosing the most effective method of forbidding her to inquire further. "If anyone likes artichokes, there are artichokes on hand. Olivia, mind that you two don't go anywhere near the windows. I'll see you shortly." The front door closed behind him.

Twenty-four

"Christ, this is awful. I know what, let's slither out the service entrance and—why not?—go down to Trunk Street and have an orgy."

This followed by Jonas's catching, careless, chuckling laugh.

The words had bothered Gus since he had heard about the taxi driver's identification of his fare and her destination.

A party at Alex Homans' apartment at the top of the Barclay, late in May, more or less a command performance, a celebration of the twenty-fifth anniversary of the founding of the agency. The entire staff was there. It was like a Christmas party, only, if possible, worse, because most of Homans' clients and their wives were there, too.

Jonas and his orgy were right behind him, at the piano. Gus himself was being lectured on the culture of azaleas by an enormous woman in an alarmingly low-cut dress. He remembered the moment and the words, because he had been tired, and bored, and wondering if he was getting drunk or whether it was the smoke and the heat and the azaleas. Jonas's suggestion—addressed to whom, he had no idea—had come sifting through a Cole Porter song Jonas was playing with style and throwaway ease, one of his own favorites, "I Concentrate on You."

". . . an acid soil is an absolute must," the enormous woman went on relentlessly. "Your oak-leaf mulch is beneficial to all azaleas, but you particularly want it for your Ghent variety. . . ."

"I can personally provide a belly dancer," Jonas continued. "I met her last night at the Egyptian Sands, and no matter what you may think about belly dancers, underneath it all, she's a very nice girl. . . ."

The azalea woman heard part of this and glared.

She moved away from contamination. Bodies shifted. Gus had been attacked by another client's wife, and in a short time he escaped and forgot for the moment all about Jonas and his proposed orgy.

Trunk Street. He had never heard of it, in his five years in Philadelphia. Either it had a club of some sort, or someone's private house or apartment suitable for bacchanalian rites. He tried again to find in his visual memory the person Jonas had been talking to, but there had been a crush of people around the piano. He did remember Aldington's neigh, close.

Too flimsy, shadowy to go to the police with; too pointed and interesting in its own vague way to be ignored, now that there was this fear, about and for Millie, rasping at him.

He got his car out of the garage down the street and drove toward the river and south, and parked it on Second Street in front of the silent garage before turning on foot into the narrow rainswept alley. A street map checked before he started showed that it ran only one block.

Representing himself without any credentials at all as Press, he had no trouble—tall and trenchcoated and emanating authority—in gaining admittance to those houses on Trunk Street occupied by their owners or tenants that night. The police had, of course, been there before him, but he could only assume their hard-pressed man or men wouldn't have been able to spend a great deal of time on one shabby block that might or might not mean anything in the case of Dora Maunder.

He worked his way up one side of the street and down the other. There was nothing that resembled a private or public club, no leaking of music, gathering of cars.

His questions were brief: had they seen or heard anything last night, and who exactly were their neighbors on either side?

An apricot negligee, slightly soiled, invited him to stay for a cup of coffee. An elderly gray-haired man asked would they be on the TV news and did he have a camera crew with him. A small boy took aim at his head with a slingshot and was snatched and held behind her by his mother.

About the middle of the block, on the north side, was a house in total darkness. There was no answer to his knock. To the left of the house was the burnt-out ruin of what had once been an identical modest old brick with marble steps. Someone had torn the marble steps away.

To its right was a shabby sister, fronted with asbestos in a hideous fieldstone pattern. The ground floor had been converted into a store, and the big dusty plate glass displayed, in the faint gleam of the streetlight at the other end of the street, a scrawl of the ubiquitous Philadelphia graffiti in white spray paint, and a For Rent sign.

Gus went along the cracked concrete driveway beside the center house to the garage at the back. Its doors were closed and padlocked. Through the streaming window, his flashlight found an empty cement floor stained with oil and grease. Nothing else, no litter of tools, old cardigan sweaters hung on hooks, crusted clay flowerpots, bicycle pumps, or any of the normal garage clutter.

He climbed the marble stairs in front and tried the window to the right of it. Locked or stuck. The flashlight was powerless against tightly drawn curtains, not filmy but opaque, of some dark material, blue or gray. Looking up, he saw all the windows were heavily curtained. Yes, a suitable place for an orgy, complete with a belly dancer.

There was a frightful din of trucks going by at the end of the street. He kept looking over his shoulder. It would be all too easy for someone to slip up behind him unheard, and he wasn't remotely interested in getting, at the very least, a blow on the back of his head.

He went back for the second time to the house across the street. A gray-haired woman with a Hungarian accent patiently answered his knock again. No, she didn't know who lived there. There didn't seem to be anyone home ever, in the daytime, or at least she'd never seen anyone. She thought she remembered hearing a car, occasionally, at night, turning in at the driveway, and the sound of the garage doors opening. She explained anxiously that she was sorry she hadn't anything to tell him, but most nights she sat in her kitchen at the back of the house watching TV. She belied the tradition of the great American all-seeing neighbor; she was obviously incurious about the heavily curtained, secret-looking brick house.

Maybe, after all, the house was untenanted. Maybe whoever entered the driveway, occasionally, at night, was the owner, checking on his premises for possible vandalism, or completing the arrangements for renting the house furnished.

Gus, restlessly prowling, strangely reluctant to leave, studied the door at right angles to the garage doors. A kitchen door, from the look of it, panes above, black-painted wood below, the same maddening all-obscuring curtains.

He took his coat off, balled his fist in its folds, and broke the lower right-hand pane. The crash sounded appallingly loud.

He could hear himself saying to a policeman, "I could swear I heard a woman screaming somewhere upstairs. I thought she might be ill or in trouble—" And see the snippet in the newspaper, "Man found housebreaking on Murder Street. Mr. Augustus Welcome apprehended by police. . . ."

His hand, twisting, found the Yale lock and snapped it, found the doorknob and turned it. He listened. The door whined a little to itself as he slipped through it and softly closed it behind him.

A small kitchen, reasonably clean. He opened the refrigerator door several inches, not wanting to let its light leak into the room. A half gallon of California Chablis. Beer, cheese, fruit, chocolates. Party food.

He wondered for a wild moment if this could be where Jonas had been and was now hiding out. Coming and going by night. It would explain the air of secrecy he felt so strongly about the house, outside and in. An obscure, muffled place. A hideaway.

But Millie had been so sure. So sure Jonas had certainly been shot, wounded, probably killed. A wounded man could, however, lie low here. Nothing to stop him calling a doctor. Get himself cleaned up, bandaged. "I'm sorry to trouble you, doctor. Like a damned fool, I didn't have the safety on. It was an accident. . . ." Wouldn't the doctor make a report to the police? Not necessarily. Paper work. Officialdom. Money-minting hours wasted.

The swinging kitchen door opened into a biggish square room, a living room. Heavy upholstered furniture, dark colorless rug, nothing that said, I live here, I'm somebody, I'm real. No open book lying on its face, no magazines, no flowers fading in their vase, no cigarette butts or ashes in the ashtrays, no flung-down newspaper. Not even that most impersonal sign of an attempt at human enjoyment, a television set.

Stairs went up a side wall. Two bedrooms, one absolutely empty, with powdery dust balls lurking in the corners. The other with a big double bed, neatly made up under anonymous white candlewick, two double sets of pillows at the head. Comfortable.

Thick round white rugs on either side of the bed. A forgotten lipstick, its cap off, a strange amber-pink, on one of the bedside tables. Faintly shining rings left by glasses. On the other bedside table, two aspirin tablets someone had forgotten to take, more drink circles, a white clock-radio. Something on the floor protruding from under the bedspread—a heartily padded pink bra, with a strong perfume breathing from it.

There was a chest of drawers, empty. The closet was empty, too, except for a few wire hangers. In the small bathroom, a robe on a hook behind the door: neuter, bone-dry, a big loose white toweling affair. In the medicine cabinet, an electric shaver, a can of April Music deodorant talcum powder, three cellophane-wrapped toothbrushes, and a tube of toothpaste. No jumble of pills, first-aid equipment, nail polish, the odds and ends that jammed most medicine cabinets.

The bedroom and bath, in their understated way, announced what this house was all about.

Forcing himself, because the heavy silence was pressing in on him, he went down the stairs, opened a door to the left of the refrigerator, and made his flashlit way down to the cellar. Clean and bare, with the cold furnace at one end, the gas water heater beside it. Turned on. At the ready for the shower, the hot bath.

Back up the creaking steps, and on into the living room where he had seen from outside the unremarkable boarded pane in the window over the driveway. No cracked glass on the inside; the glass had been neatly removed. A few specks of it twinkled up at him from the floor beneath.

The telephone sat on a table desk against the kitchen wall of the room. There was a battered captain's chair at the desk. Gus went and sat down in it, his back to the kitchen door, and thoughtfully fingered the telephone. Given a slight slouch or lean to the left, a man sitting here, with this phone, was in a direct line between the kitchen door and the boarded-up windowpane.

Jonas, drunk or close to it on champagne, on the phone. Saying, if Millie's recollections were correct, that he didn't want to trouble someone whose name sounded like Farnall, but that when Farnall heard what he had to say . . .

Someone listening from the kitchen, or overhearing while he—or she—opened a beer or mixed a drink or got out food. Then the move to the doorway, the shot, to stop, temporarily or forever, the utterance of a statement.

The bullet would without much doubt have buried itself in the burnt-out house next door.

This chair. This telephone. Someone had wiped it with oil that smelled lemony. His flashlight, inquiringly fingering the floor beneath and around the chair, found only shabby linoleum patterned in a dim gray-on-gray mottle, like rain or tears. The edge of the colorless rug lay two feet from the chair leg. The linoleum was clean and lightly waxed.

There was a sound from the street immediately outside. He snapped off the flashlight and moved to the window. The curtains made an implacable dark barrier. He fingered the curtain a fraction of an inch open on one side. Enough to show him a man standing quite still in the center of the narrow cobbled street, staring at the house. Aldington. His white linen jacket caught a dim glow from the streetlight. He was frowning. Had he seen the infinitesimal tweak of the curtain? He reached into his pocket and took something out and bent his head, regarding it thoughtfully. A gun, small, slim, just about the size of his open palm.

Gus had no intention of engineering a confrontation with Aldington's nasty-looking little gun. Another time, another place, when the odds were slightly more even.

He moved silently back to the kitchen door and kept his hand on the knob. The moment the front door opened, he would make a very rapid exit. A portion of a second was all that would be needed to get across the driveway and into the yawning window of the blackened house, if cover was necessary.

The front door didn't open. Gus waited, with tension-stiffened muscles, for ten minutes by his watch. Maybe, he thought, he had dismissed too quickly the idea of Jonas hiding here. Unreal as it was, here was he, a respectable citizen, occupation art director, skulking against the door of a house he had unlawfully broken into, hiding from an equally respectable, if to him personally detestable, television show host. It gave him a much clearer idea of the topsy-turvy world Millie had been inhabiting for days.

Then he heard the sound of a car driving slowly up the street and turning out of it, going north. A distinctive sound, a Jaguar without mufflers. Aldington had a Jaguar. It was a familiar sight on the better streets of Philadelphia. Old and black and beautifully cared for and arrogantly noisy.

He went out the kitchen door and made a cautious trip down the driveway. The street was empty. Thunder cracked abruptly and the rain started again.

Twenty-five

Cane, who considered most volunteered male information, as against female, usually sound, and who was further reassured by the strong crisp sound of the other man's voice, listened with interest to Gus, calling from a phone booth on Blenheim Court.

Gus played a few tricks with the truth. He would not offer his theories about a windowpane lined up with a telephone and a kitchen doorway to the police. They had the equipment and the techniques; let them find out who lived in the muffled house and what had happened there.

He said that he worked with Jonas at Homans, and knew he often went down to a house on Trunk Street; whose house it was he had no idea. "I broke into the house, I thought Jonas might be recovering from a two- or three-day party, and perhaps, shall we say, incapacitated," he said innocently. "I happened to look out of the window, and Aldington was standing directly outside, with a gun in his hand. It's a pretty funny coincidence, don't you think, when Dora Maunder for no reason anyone can figure out got out of her cab at Trunk Street?"

He had considered going to Aldington himself, but decided against it. People who shot people on impulse, during telephone calls, might have a nervous readiness to pick up their weapons again.

"Mmm," Cane said. "It is funny, although—"

The although meant, Who's kidding who. We all know why the woman probably died. For nothing. Nothing at all.

"—it wouldn't hurt to see who lives in the house, and why Aldington was outside it with his gun. We knew, by the way, he had one—

who hasn't? You say you know Rath. You really think there's some hookup here?"

"Yes. I do."

"Oh, well," Cane said tiredly, "*hell*."

"Of course I can explain, my dear detective," Aldington said. "But I do hope you won't go around blabbing about it, as it's rather a secret at the moment."

They were in his office at KGW. A tape of one of his "Good Morning" shows was running on a monitor on the wall behind Cane; Aldington could be heard, voice volume down, talking about the Devon Horse Show.

He alternately watched Cane's face and his own face on the monitor. He paused occasionally in his monologue to relish some especially fine bit of Aldingtonia.

"I'm doing a filmed show on this thing. 'A Death in Philadelphia,' or, 'An Everyday Murder,' something like that. I don't believe it's ever been done, at least the way I plan it, a kind of documentary. The fascination would lie in the daily *ordinariness* of disaster. Murder coming around as regularly, and monotonously, as the morning milk used to—before, alas, our day. But spreading its little circles of pain in little gray lives. I'll get inside the apartment and show Maunder's pathetic little possessions. Shots of the funeral—one could wish for rain, for the right atmosphere. Mourning relatives, the sister and her husband. Interviews with her friends, 'She was a great pal,' and so on. Stills of her when she was young. Homicide Detective Cane, going efficiently about his business. Maybe a sidelight on *your* home, family, hobbies—we discover you are queer for tropical fish."

He laughed at the power of his own invention and took a full minute to light his pipe.

"A reconstruction of the actual murder, night scene, murderer of course shadowy, unidentified. 'This is how it happened that dark night. . . .' And X marks the spot in Elfreth's Alley. A whole lot more I won't bore you with. And then, of course, it would be wonderful if one—one's cameras, rather—could be in at the kill when the murderer was found, caught, and either taken away in handcuffs or killed, as they so often—accidentally—are."

Cane thought there was something greedy and fevered, something unpleasant about Aldington's excitement.

Hell of a good cover, if you had been the man who had done it.

"And the gun in your hand?"

"Well, I read about the taxi driver and her getting out at Trunk Street. I drove down there to try to get the feel of the street, look for camera angles and so on, study the time of day we'd want to shoot it. Nasty, sinister little street, by the way. I came upon this curtained-up dark house about the center of the block and was just standing there, thinking it would make a lovely house for someone to be murdered in, when I saw a curtain twitch. Not a light, not a sound from the house, but the curtain couldn't have tweaked itself at the edge, could it? Having no intention of submitting to a possible armed attack from inside, I just got out my gun and held it and studied it. To let the tweaker, as it were, know it was there, and he'd better not try anything."

He paused to smile at himself on the wall.

"And then?"

"Oh, I stood there a bit, and went around the corner and into the drive, and listened—interesting coincidence, the house, all those curtains, but probably nothing, a recluse, an invalid trying to shut out those appalling truck noises—and then I got into my car and drove innocently and anticlimactically here to the office."

"Just for the record, where were you Wednesday night about midnight?"

"Oh, an alibi, what fun! I believe I told you before. I was working on my columns for 'Aldington's U.S.A.' I went to bed about two o'clock. And no, there was no one else there. I'm afraid you'll have to take it on trust."

He gave Cane his lip-lift smile.

"—and could one possibly hope the police would notify one when they're closing in on the culprit? It would do *you* some good, you know, hero of the hour—"

"I'm afraid not, Mr. Aldington."

"What you're saying is that you people will probably never find out who did it and why. Well, one can always try the Commissioner."

Routine police inquiries turned up the fact that the house on Trunk Street was owned by a Nicholas Oforio. He was a retired man, a widower, now traveling by car in Italy. His sister in South Philadelphia rather thought he had sublet the house. She wasn't sure about the sublet, but she said a skinflint like her brother wouldn't let it go begging when there was money to be got out of it. "If I were you I wouldn't go looking for a lease. Probably strictly cash—he don't do his personal business on paper. He's due back any day now, you can talk to him yourself."

Bell of Pennsylvania was contacted and asked if they would go through their records, or ask their computers to do so, with the following object: find out from what subscriber had a call been made to Millicent Lester's number in New York early in the morning on June the second. "You don't know the name of the party calling?" a voice asked in a stunned way. "Do you know how many telephones there are in this city? Of course, we'll do our best—"

But soon after these activities were undertaken, the house on Trunk Street no longer seemed of the least importance.

Twenty-six

Until she had bathed and brushed her teeth and gotten into the big bed, Millie didn't realize the edge of terror that she had been living on.

Listening, back in the magenta and brown hotel room, trying for sleep, to every footfall in the corridor—would the sounds stop at her door? Would the knob turn?

And waking suddenly, with a startled heart—a telephone in the next room, an ambulance or fire engine in the street, more footsteps in an out-of-control stagger—

And the night thoughts, the dark and terrible night thoughts . . . racing, uncontrollable—

Gus's corner bedroom's most valuable furniture was peace and safety. She lay with the lights on, luxuriating for a few minutes in the temporary lifting of a heavy load. A pretty room, a woman's room. Parrot-patterned chintz over white batiste underskirts at the tall windows, a soft yellow and apricot Persian rug, the bed and chest of drawers old and enameled a rosy ivory and painted with butterflies. A well-filled bookcase, a great long cushiony chair murmuring of afternoon naps.

Olivia, when Gus had returned, repaired immediately to Jonas's quarters. "It was nice being off duty for a bit. Your lamb chops were very good." At the front door, she turned. "Millie, I forgot to tell you. This morning I found a fifty-thousand-dollar life insurance policy. You're the beneficiary. He must have forgotten to change it. On your demise, I get what's left. If—" briskly opening the door—"he's remembered to keep up with the premiums, which I very much doubt."

Gus smiled faintly when the door closed behind her. "Businesslike sort of woman, isn't she?"

"I think," Millie said, "it's her way of keeping her head above water. Just as you do mine." She looked at him with deep gratitude and without knowing it, a great deal more than that. She shone at him. "Shall I get you some dinner?"

He said nothing about his evening's errand and she asked no questions.

I have a private life, remember?

She sat with him while he ate his chop and New Jersey beefsteak tomatoes and her special hashed brown potatoes.

"Leave the dishes, Millie. Go on up to bed. I have a nice woman who comes in at eleven every day and potters about."

His presence, his life, his house, his habits folding about her like eiderdown. For a few short hours. She said, "Good night, then, Gus," and he said, "Well, almost," and she went obediently up the stairs. She thought, on her way to the corner room, it must be his bedroom she was passing, right at the head of the stairs.

Door half open, comfortable brandy-brown air to it, another Persian rug, amber and blue, a watercolor—his?—swift and vivid, a row of doves on a bare angling branch, over the leather headboard of the broad bed. Open book on the table beside it. Unable to resist, she went closer to the watercolor and found his initials in pencil in the corner.

It must have been no longer than five minutes after her bath water had stopped running out when the light knock sounded on her door.

She had been thinking, with determined admiration, how surprising, how pleasant it was, that a man like Gus Welcome would take you in under his roof, no one else here at all, and—

Leave you alone.

"Don't panic, Millie," he said, opening the door and coming in. He wore a blue and white striped robe. His feet were bare. "I'm going to sleep in your long chair, if you don't mind." He stood a few feet from her and looked down at her, her well-brushed hair and soap-polished skin and her eyes, very wide, fastened to his.

"I hate to put you out," she said politely.

"Put me out—? Oh, you mean inconvenience me. Don't worry. It's a very comfortable chair."

He went around the room checking the latches on the long windows.

Then he went to the large painted armoire at the other side of the bed, opened it, and took out a light blanket.

"Is your pillow all right for you? Too hard? Or too soft? There are others in here—"

"No, it's just right."

"Would you like the air conditioning down or up?"

"No, it's fine."

"By the way," he said, tossing the blanket on the chair, "if you'd like to call Mike Garland in Rome, go ahead. Just because I've shut you in, I don't want you to feel yourself deprived of your civil rights. I have to go and get a book anyway. You won't mind one light, low, if I read for a while?"

"No, of course not—they'll be comforting, the book and the light, I mean," and again, polite, "I don't think I will call, thank you. But thank you anyway."

She was very much aware of her bare shoulders but didn't want to pull up the protecting sheet. Not the correct gesture for this neighborly manner of his.

"You look awfully wide awake, Millie," he said, coming over to the side of the bed and looking down at her again. "Maybe you'd like some aspirin, or a hot drink of something. . . ."

"Nothing, thank you."

For God's sake stop saying thank you. "You do loom a bit, you know. I'm sure I'll be sleepy when you settle down—"

"Well, that's good. I'll be back in a minute or two."

The bedroom regained its breath when he left it and then lost it again when he came back in. His presence filled the room, pushed back the walls and heightened the ceiling, and made the very air shake as though music was playing at full strength.

Trying to look serene and sensibly, amiably protected by a kind friend, Millie, now thoroughly sheeted, reclined against her pillows.

He went around turning off lamps. Fingers on the switch of the one beside her, he said thoughtfully, "I would like very much to kiss you good night. I don't think it would be a good idea, do you?"

"No," Millie said. Nice if she could manage a relaxed smile, worldly. A woman thoroughly in charge of herself, amused, accepting her unlikely situation. She couldn't. A nervous quiver caught her underlip at one corner. She bit it away.

He left one light on, low, as promised, and stretched out in the long chair and opened his book.

Turn over, away from him, away from the light, on her other side, and try to sleep? That would look rude, perhaps. She decided against her right side, split the difference and lay on her back and was sharply aware of the lift of her breasts under the pink and white flowered sheet.

Lashes lowered, eyes almost closed, she studied the butterflies on the tall chest.

Gus was very quiet, one knee up under his blanket, supporting his book, one long leg extended. The light touched a hard elegant cheekbone and the strong jut of his nose, the long face crease on the left-hand side looking now, not amused, but tense.

He seemed, in the lamplight, younger than she had yet seen him, and a little pale. As she watched, he lifted his eyes from his book and looked at her, a long piercing gray glance sending an almost touchable surge of warmth at her.

Either, she thought. Or.

Either they might, someday, strange lovely idea, look back and laugh, ". . . you in that chair . . . and I didn't know which way to lie. I thought you'd be offended by my back. . . . What on *earth*, now that I think of it, were you reading . . . ?"

Or, the bitter certainty all the rest of her life, I blew it. I passed that particular ship in the night. I blew it. . . . *I once knew this marvelous man in Philadelphia, oh, years ago . . . but I was terribly mixed up at the time, you see, and . . .*

But no, not as clear-cut as that. There was a middle ground that was a quivering uncertain place to stand on. Gus, I can't bear to be here while you're there. I want you.

Do you? Sorry. I thought we'd been through all that. What you feel may be fake, remember?

Well, but Gus, just this once, I'll be on my way—

But could I ever get back to where I'm going, or think I'm going, after you?

Okay, Millie, if it's a nice warm body you want, move over. Why not? But you know, you don't have to keep *thanking* me if that's what's behind your kind offer. . . .

You must understand, Gus, that I know this isn't any kind of commitment, for you, this is a nice casual sort of thing that people do, people who are attracted to each other.

I am *not* saying, not out loud, not at least to you, I can't ever go ahead, now, with Mike Garland, I want you, not just for tonight, but for good. . . .

He gave a long sigh, to himself, and turned out the lamp beside him.

She called on all the courage she had.

"Gus . . ."

"Yes, Millie?"

"Will you, please, come here, to me?"

"To kiss you good night?" He was already on his feet.

"If you want to. All night."

Against the dim light coming in at the window, she saw him, tall, approaching, a winglike motion as he shed his robe. He lifted the sheet and very slowly and carefully and strongly moved in against her and turned her body to his. She heard him half whispering, as if in pain, "Christ, Millie darling . . . my love, my— I was wondering if you'd ever . . . *ever*—" The rest was lost as his mouth took hers.

Waking to a kiss on her shoulder, somewhere near dawn, she murmured, without indignation, "Gus, you played me like a piano."

". . . in what particular way?"

". . . waiting there. So patiently, but looking so deep in your book, until I—"

"I wanted you to make your choice, make up your own mind. Quietly."

"*Quietly!*"

"—it may be very firm-jawed and manly, striding in and taking over a territory, but there's not much point in claiming a woman who doesn't want to be claimed."

He turned on the lamp, raised himself on one elbow and studied the face a few inches below his own. How delightful, she thought, not to fear and have to turn away from the ultimate intimacy, gaze buried in gaze, self buried in self, without defenses or evasions of any kind.

"When I said, make your choice, I meant just that," he said. "I hope and trust you don't think I'm borrowing you?"

For a moment she was confused. Not really borrowing her, just having a night with her—?

He laughed a little under his breath. "If you want it spelled out, this is your second engagement announcement this year—or rather the first celebration of your marriage." Into her throat, and her bloodstream, ". . . did you ever really think I had any intention of letting you go?"

He fingered away tears under her eyes. "Don't, Millie."

She pulled his head down to her and said gaspingly, "I know there may still be things to . . . weep about . . . but I feel like a plane with one engine out and the undercarriage stuck that's come safely in on the runway anyway."

Twenty-seven

He almost fell on a Mrs. Nobile, a waitress who had just gone, after her night's work, through the restaurant's back door into the narrow alley between Sixteenth and Seventeenth behind Walnut Street.

There was a scream as from an eagle far above and then a disastrous crash and explosion and spill of bone and blood, muscle, brain, life, humanity.

Mrs. Nobile fled howling like an animal from it—the man was not now *he*, but *it*.

"Eeeeeee—eeeeeeee . . . !"

This section of town—glossy, good shops, Bonwit Teller up at the corner to her right, the Warwick a few blocks south—was well patrolled. A police car drew up beside her. A window was rolled down.

The patrolman got, between her heaving sobs and cries, her hand holding her heart as though to keep it from flying out of her body, "—a man—though I don't know, with pants suits—down that alley—a man—"

Unlike newer buildings with sealed windows, the building Homans occupied had long ago installed air conditioning, but the big double-hung windows still opened.

As was immediately visible when the police entered Shattner's office.

Also immediately visible was the long and detailed confession in his typewriter.

He had, he said, on a sudden violent impulse, shot and killed an associate at Homans, Jonas Rath. Rath had been threatening him, "demanding outrageous sums of money for a house he had suddenly decided he needed," and he had taken advantage of the turned back when Rath called someone on the telephone. The murder had taken place at the small pool cabana-house at his home in Strafford. It was late; they were, he wrote, both drinking, and added that he could not set down his reasons for killing Rath because innocent people would be damaged.

He gave exact instructions as to where to find the body.

". . . following his directions," the voice on the radio in the sunny kitchen said, as Gus casually flicked it on, "within hours the Pennsylvania State Police went down Loader's Lane, located the three pine stumps, and after kicking aside a heap of dead scrub dug and found the body of Philadelphia advertising executive Jonas Rath—"

Millie hurled herself at Gus.

Stunned, he held the shuddering body tightly and said, "But you knew, Millie, you knew, you said you knew. . . ."

"I know, but it's not the same as knowing," Millie said in a stricken whisper.

He referred to Dora Maunder as "that bitch," which appeared more primly in the newspapers as "that woman."

"She chose to occupy herself exclusively with finding out where Jonas was or what had happened to him. I had no way of knowing whether Jonas had told her certain facts about my private life. They were neighbors or friends. I thought how ridiculous it would be if after all I had gone through she could in her turn destroy me."

He had driven over in his car, he said, to see her late Wednesday night, but just as he was turning into Cypress Street he saw her come out of her apartment. He followed her cab.

"She got out at a street far downtown and began walking up it. I came up behind her, taking her by surprise, and I said I wanted to talk to her, and we walked to my car. I probed a little, and found out what she did know, and she laughed about it in a terrible hysterical way, and I then strangled her."

"'I then,'" screamed Ellen McGuire. "Like a business memo or something . . . 'I then, I *then* . . . !'"

"I was thinking to drive to the woods again but for some reason I panicked with her there in the car, I didn't think I could afford the risk of stopping the car and putting her in the trunk. I stopped at the entrance to a dark little alleyway and put her over the fence there, into some weeds or bushes."

" 'A dark little alleyway,' " Cane said. "He only picks the most famous little alley in Philadelphia, is all."

The prose style of the rest of Shattner's confession grew a little confused and emotional, a wandering of words possibly not unconnected with the open bottle of whiskey on his desk, half empty.

Neither the *Bulletin* nor the *Inquirer* printed this portion, but one of the tabloids, which had a man who had a connection with a girl at police headquarters who could manage a forbidden Xerox, did.

Under a headline DEAD MAN FINDS VICTIM'S EX WIFE RESPONSIBLE FOR DOUBLE DEATHS, "I wish to accuse Millicent Rath of Dora Maunder's death and in a way of my own. If she had not come here making trouble none of this would have happened. She wasn't even married to the bastard any more. I tried in my own way once, but (a series of x'd-out words). Goddamn all nosy women! I hired a man to follow her and try to scare her off. I sent her through the mail a note to me from Jonas, the kind of note he always wrote me, telling her—me—to go to hell, which I heartily hope she does. But the bloody bitch just dug in like a maggot."

The two-page document ended with a few flat sad wrenching words. "In spite of everything, I do really love you, Alma."

"I'd better go upstairs to Olivia," Millie said. "She'll have heard. She's all alone."

She found Olivia sitting on the black leather sofa holding a long opened envelope.

"His salary check," Olivia said. "It came in the morning mail. And I've just had a call from the dentist's office. Apparently this girl doesn't read the papers or listen to the radio. She wanted to know if Jonas was going to be able to keep his appointment tomorrow, and I said, I hardly think so, under the circumstances, and she said, I wish you could be more accurate—doctor's time is valuable."

And then her face cracked open.

Twenty-eight

Millie thought it a little strange that Gus did not go with her to Dora's funeral mass. He said there was a meeting at Homans he absolutely couldn't skip. But he had always, during this timeless and terrible week, been so firmly, so unmistakably *there*.

Perhaps he was one of those people who couldn't face the trappings and ceremonies of death. Odd that you could love a man and at the same time not really know him well.

The mass was low, short, and unembellished. Millie could see the little group of Dora's immediate relatives in the front pews, and then pew after pew of people who could only have come for the spectacle of a murdered woman's funeral service, and who could have found after all little to regale themselves with in the quiet voice of the black-vestmented priest and the plain dark coffin between its candles.

She had been surprised to see, just before the mass started, Jim Ryan come in at a side door, and slip into a pew near the rear of the church. He saw her glancing at him and gave her a faint, we're-in-church smile.

". . . Grant, we pray, Almighty God, that the soul of your servant Dora Maunder which has departed out of this world . . ."

That other funeral. Jonas's. After whatever the police did when they found murdered, buried bodies— She gripped the shining rounded wooden top of the pew in front of her.

Now the priest was swinging the censer toward Dora's coffin. Fragrant smoke drifted. She stared straight ahead of her when the coffin, followed by the family, went by. An indecency, to look into their faces.

She had called Flo Grattle, asking if she was going to the funeral and whether she was going on to the cemetery. Flo said yes to both questions and offered a ride in her car. "We don't know each other, but company's a help at a time like this."

She had been up in front, behind the family. She was waiting, red-eyed, on the church steps as Millie came out.

"Only forty-three," Flo Grattle said, starting to cry again. "My car's around the corner. Only forty-three. And she was a good egg. —I hope to God you don't take seriously what that madman said about you being responsible."

"No," Millie said. "No, not really, no, I don't think I do . . . no . . ." She wished for tears but something had locked her face shut.

"And you're completely satisfied?" Gus had asked Cane over the phone.

"Christ almighty, man! Yes, we're satisfied. We've got a body and a confession and a wrap-up. Did you happen to catch the daily crime count in yesterday's paper? Only one hundred and twenty-nine major crimes reported, that's all— What's your gripe?"

"That house," Gus said. "The house on Trunk Street. There was no mention of it, unless you held it back, censored it."

"No, we didn't. That's only been a hunch of yours all along, a guess. You guessed wrong."

"Did you take time out from your hundred-plus crimes to look at Shattner's cabana?"

Cane, who had been up all night, was inclined to snarl. "Of course. There's a cement floor that gets hosed down every day by one of the kids. We didn't find a bullet, but the place is lousy with sliding doors and windows. If you've done your reading lesson right, he threw the gun away in the woods, remember? We haven't found it."

"And won't now—why bother?"

"Yes," Cane said. "Exactly."

Gus found himself severely tempted, like Cane, to leave it alone. Let the wretched Shattner carry the blame into his grave. But old crimes could stir in their sleep.

A year from now, ten years from now . . .

The June rain fell on the priest, the mourners, the mound of flowers on the tactful green carpet covering heaped earth. It fell on Aldington, with his hand-held camera, all but hidden behind a stout stone angel with outspread wings.

Joe McGuire saw the hands, and the camera, as he turned from the open grave to steer his wife to the long black car.

"Do you suppose she'll be on the television news or a special feature or something?" he asked. "That was Aldington, I'm sure of it."

Jim Ryan stood beside the car waiting for the McGuires. It had been made clear to the uncles and cousins and aunt that there was to be no post-funeral feasting. Not after a death like this. A murder. The murderer himself freshly dead.

"I'm going to take you two to a quiet lunch," Ryan said. "Think of it as Homans' tribute to Dora. After all, eighteen years. I regret the falling out, I do indeed. I'll tell the man to drive to the Barclay, shall I? I have a private room ready."

Gus left his car in Blenheim Court, walked along Second Street with the rain spitting at him, and turned up Trunk Street. Dirty brooks ran in the cobblestoned gutters. A woman at the other end of the street, struggling with an umbrella and a loaded shopping cart, maneuvered herself up stained marble steps and disappeared behind a peeling dark red door, the color of old dried blood.

At number 217, the kitchen door windowpane he had broken had not been replaced. He reached through and unlocked the door and went into the muffled silent house and stood listening, not just with his ears but with every pore of his body.

Nothing. Nothing but the rattle of rain on the tin roof of the garage.

He went quietly, carefully over the house, upstairs, down into the cellar. As far as he could judge, the food in the refrigerator had not been touched. The bathrobe still hung dry on its hook behind the door.

After he had completed his tour, he went into the living room, took off his raincoat and sat down in one of the shabby armchairs. He had a newspaper and a paperback. Hard to read in the gloom, but he couldn't afford the light. It was ten-thirty. Dora's funeral mass, he thought, would be just starting.

He was prepared to be patient.

It might be days.

Or, it might just be a matter of hours.

At the Warwick, Millie and Flo Grattle had a single joyless drink; they attempted determined forkfuls of shrimp Lamaze. It was a late lunch. The dining room was emptying. Flo talked about Dora and Millie listened, with an occasional guilty mental straying to Gus. It was necessary to wrap herself in him for a moment, now and then, this sad dark pouring day.

After coffee, Flo said, "Can I drop you anywhere? I'm due back at work, but first I have to go to Wanamaker's to buy vacuum cleaner bags. Funny kind of thing to have to do on the heels of a funeral, isn't it? Life, as they say, goes on."

She had strict orders from Gus to join Olivia at Jonas's apartment. Flo drove her there and as Millie got out of the car said, "Oh, I forgot you have another funeral—or something—ahead of you. I'm so sorry—"

"That's all right," Millie said, foolish with fatigue, "and thank you, Flo."

There was a note on the white door at the top of the stairs. "You know what, under front leg of chair nearest door." The key.

How silent the apartment was. There would be no more phone calls that would send the heart jumping. No more need to check his mail and see to his laundry and drinking water. And no more listening for footsteps on the stairs. Running quickly, gay, hopeful always —Jonas.

The phone did ring, and the fear which had become a habit reinstated itself.

It was Olivia.

"I'm breaking a promise," Olivia said. "But I didn't actually promise, and things are too terrible now for good manners. I don't know what's gotten into your friend and protector Gus Welcome. He called this morning and said if I didn't hear from him by five o'clock to call that man Cane and get him down to—he gave me the number

—a house on Trunk Street. He said under no circumstances was I to tell you about it. I said why the secrecy, everything's all over with, and he said I wish it was but I don't think it is—and you know, Millie, I have rather a high idea of that man's intelligence—" Then she added something which Millie didn't remember till later, because her puzzled concern was turning into something far worse. "We both seem to be setting ourselves up as traps. It's a now-or-never thing, I suppose."

Twenty-nine

At a little after three on what seemed the longest day of his life, there was a faint sound at the kitchen door.

He had left it unlocked. He got up and went silently to stand against a wall a few feet from the doorway that led into the kitchen. The swinging door was open. He had no weapon, except the weapon of surprise, and his own strength to call on.

Whoever it was was hesitating just inside the kitchen, assessing, probably, the broken pane, the unlocked door. Robbery was such a daily commonplace that this need give him, Gus thought, no overwhelming cause for alarm.

Moving lightly, raincoated and wearing a dashing and concealing hat whose wide turned-down brim hid the telltale red hair, Jim Ryan walked into the living room in a careful, tentative way, tossed an attaché case on the couch, and spun and staggered and almost fell when Gus's cool voice said, "Planting something of Shattner's?"

Ryan was staring at him as though he was totally unable to believe his eyes. His cheerful milkmaid color had vanished.

Then Ryan laughed, a high snorting sound.

"You've got it all wrong, fella." He took off his hat and threw it on the couch beside the attaché case. "Today is my day for good works. I've just been to Dora's funeral. Then I took the worthy McGuires to lunch and helped them drown their sorrows in Bourbon. Speaking of that, he keeps a bottle here—don't jump me, fella. I'll just get it out of the desk and we can both have a drink. Jesus, you really gave me a scare."

Was there, perhaps, a gun in the desk? Or in a pocket of his rain-coat?

As Ryan moved to the desk, Gus moved beside him, only inches away, ready.

Ryan pulled open the slanting desk front, took out a half-full bottle, screwed off the cap, tipped up the bottle, and drank thirstily. The smell of scotch pierced the air.

"Shot for you?"

"Thanks, I will," Gus said. He took the bottle and held it by the neck, put it back on the desk and kept his hand on it.

". . . well, anyway, as I say, my day for good works. Alma Shattner, God bless her, has enough to face without knowing about this little setup of Amos's. When the two of us moved down here from New York, the real estate man who handled the Pennsylvania properties—Oforio—was in a mood to do favors. Amos took this place under another name. He'd bring his—friends here. A terrible curse, a sad secret thing—" Ryan grinned, showing big confident teeth. "I'll take women any day, won't you? But if she ever found out about it, good-bye money, good-bye kids, good-bye Alma. I thought I'd just check the place, be sure there wasn't anything here to connect him with it. Only one chance in a hundred the police would be interested at this stage of the game, but who knows? Alma might stumble on a canceled check to Oforio or something— and why take the chance? You might call this visit my last rites for good old Amos."

Gus looked at his hand on the scotch bottle.

The smooth glib slightly drunken voice filled him with outrage.

"You're consistent, anyway," he said. "You confessed everything else for Shattner, and now you're confessing this for him. This house. What you describe as his friends. Your house. Your friends, female we'll assume, as you'll take women any day. Your windowpane—" he gestured with his head, "that had to be cut out because there was a bullet hole in it. After the bullet went through Jonas."

Ryan turned a strange dark red. He laughed, again the snorting sound.

Then he said, "Prove it."

Stalemate.

He had no proof whatever, only his instinct. Leaving aside his be-lated acceptance of Millie's theory, he thought that the fuming, put-upon Shattner was totally incapable of two murders and one suicide. That the brutality and speed and daring of the crimes was much more consistent with the buccaneering character of a Ryan. And that only Ryan was close enough to Shattner, knew enough about him and his ways, his very tone of voice, to write a convincing confession for him. A very able piece of creative copywriting.

"I will," he said. "Just give me time, you murdering bastard."

"Take all the time in the world, fella," Ryan said, with a sort of ghastly airiness. "The whole story—the whole sad story of Amos—is going to be underground in a day or so. Another funeral—I suppose we'll both have to go. I know you're fostering that bottle to hit me with if necessary, but now that we've reached an agreement, I sup-pose you don't mind if I have a wee sup?"

He got cigarettes out of his shirt pocket and lit one with a large calmed hand.

"Speaking of funerals, do you know the one about the Irishman on his deathbed who gave his best friend a vial of twenty-year-old whiskey, to pour over his coffin as a sort of benediction when it was lowered into the grave, and his friend said, 'Fine, Mike, but d'you mind if I pass it through my kidneys first?'"

Gus poured liquor into the bottle cap and handed it to him. He watched Ryan silently as he scowled at the half-ounce offering and then drank it. He felt the flow of the other man's returning confidence and steadied nerve.

What if I'm wrong? he thought. What if this brash, glib, slippery man is telling the truth? As his own guardian tension began to relax, he felt a bitter weariness and doubt coming over him.

There were people who could make the clearest truths sound eva-sive, inventive.

Perhaps no one would ever know what the truth was. Or, until or unless someone else got in Jim Ryan's way.

There was a faint whine and creak from the kitchen and then a merry burst of whistling.

"Shenandoah."

In the shadowy doorway, a tall lounging figure, hands in pockets, appeared. Gold lion locks wet and tossed. Wraparound sunglasses catching the dim light from the one lamp. Trenchcoat collar turned up jauntily. Strong mouth o'd in the whistling, cheeks drawn in, taut and shining.

Ryan crashed to his knees.

"Mother of God!" he shouted. "You're dead. *Dead . . .*"

He fumbled in his raincoat pocket and there was a shattering noise as he fired. In the seconds of fumbling, the figure had melted from the doorway.

Gus dived for his gun hand and tore the pistol away from him. Ryan clambered to his feet, looking like a man in a nightmare.

"Did . . . did you see that?" he asked, very slowly.

"See what?"

Gus felt a tremendous inward shaking, but his voice was mild and level.

Wait a minute.

"Jonas" could whistle, of course, but not speak. Not in that low womanly voice of hers. And could only afford to flicker across the retina, as she had, and then immediately vanish.

"In the doorway. Jonas Rath."

"No," Gus said. "There's no one here but you and me."

"Did you hear him, then? Whistling? A favorite of his. 'Shenandoah' . . . 'A-cross the wide Miss-ouri,'" Ryan sang in a cracked off-key voice.

Gus managed a short hard laugh. "No. I missed that. Maybe you need another drink."

Ryan was still staring at the doorway.

Beginning to speak very rapidly, he said, "I am the next president of an advertising agency. I've made it big. I go to church every Sunday. I have a grand big new house with stables, and I'm looking into the purchase of a horse or two. I have two boys, both in the best schools, both terrific football material, great guys both of them. Goosey and I have a good strong marriage. If I need more, and take it—I'm a lusty fella, I admit it—where's the harm if she doesn't know it? Goosey loves the house, and the country club, and being able to shop at Nan Duskin's. It makes up for my night and weekend work. . . ."

Telling his personal beads, Gus thought. Placing Jim Ryan in a real, believable world. Establishing, to himself, his sanity.

From somewhere—the cellar?—the faintest lilting sound. "Across the wide Missouri . . ."

"*No!*" Ryan roared. "No, I'm not going to live with him for the rest of my life—"

He leaped savagely at Gus and his square frantic hands gripped Gus's throat, thumbs speaking of death. Gus, a strong man himself, wrenched at the iron wrists, but his sane strength was not quite up to the desperate violence of the other man's.

"You saw him." A panting scream. "Say you saw him—you saw Jonas Rath—you heard him—"

Thirty

From the end of Trunk Street, Millie heard the sound of the shot.

She ran in a wild undirected way, ran for Gus's life. Which house? Oh God, which house—?

She stumbled on the wet cobblestones and nearly fell. A blue delivery van screeched to a halt behind her and the driver bellowed, "For Christ's sake, lady, don't they use sidewalks where you come from?"

The noise of the van, going down the alley, almost made her head burst. She couldn't hear, she had no way of placing the sound of the shot—

From the house on her left came a voice inhumanly demanding, rising to screaming pitch—"You saw him—you saw Jonas Rath—"

She tore at the handle of the front door, and sobbing to herself ran to the side of the house, saw the kitchen door slightly open and plunged through, and almost fell over the two men in mortal combat on the living room floor.

The blinding light of terror guided her eyes to the pistol on the desk. She seized it in both hands and bent and held it against Ryan's head. Her hands were shaking dangerously.

Ryan felt the tremor of steel against his skull, wrenched free, stared with horrified bloodshot eyes at the trembling gun and the white face above it.

"Jesus God," he shouted. "No, no, don't—what do you want? What is it you want? I thought I killed Jonas, and the others, but he's alive, so maybe I didn't, it's all—there wasn't any funeral this morning—"

and, one knee on the floor, he burst into a terrible sobbing that filled the room, the house, the world.

Gus saw and heard through a dark seething haze. Another face, high above him, in the doorway, Jonas-Olivia's? He managed to get to his feet, leaned against the desk, took the gun from Millie. He tried to speak and couldn't. She said, "Yes, I'll call Cane."

Aldington was quite smug about having bugged the house. "Living room *and* bedroom, just in case," he said. "I thought there might be action of some kind, at that house. For my little documentary. What a sound track, the pantings and groanings, and the *whistling*. . . . When you're through with that tape, my dear copper, I want it for a wedding present for somebody who was ever so curious about what really happened to Jonas Rath."

Gus had been correct. Amos Shattner's confession was in effect Ryan's confession. Only Trunk Street needed to be added to it. "Well, yes, a man set about with family and business cares has to have a pad in town," Ryan said. "A mattress pad, you might call it." In the face of total wreckage, he was quite jaunty about it all. Cane wondered about his sanity, but then no man who killed three times was sane. Three times and a fairly close fourth.

He and the fairly close fourth victim had taken a liking to each other. When Gus, through Millie, issued an invitation to a late Sunday morning breakfast, Cane said, "Why not?"

On his arrival at the house on Delancey Street, Gus whispered huskily, "Salvatore Cane. Save the dogs."

"You're Welcome."

With this exchange, the two men went through the hall to the back garden. It was filled, after the days of rain and heat, with crystal sunlight and indigo-black shadow, racing and trembling over the whitewashed walls, and white petunias and a white-dressed Millie.

She perched, hands loosely clasped about her knees, on a blue and white Chinese porcelain garden seat. When the sun floated on her hair, it found lavender shimmers. She looked at one moment lost and tired, at another young and beautifully lighted up. Cane felt a brief pang of envy. He wouldn't wonder if she hadn't spent the night

here, to comfort her love. That would explain the shining look that
came and went, he thought.

She got up and went to a white table laden festively with hot
coffee and food, a tub of ice, bottles, the makings for bloody marys.

As they drank coffee, Gus croaked, "Now. Everything. Both on
the record and off. Particularly as we loomed large in the cast, at the
end."

"Don't talk, Gus," Millie said. Every word he spoke tore her
throat.

Cane had an accurate vocal memory. About Shattner, Ryan said:

"Well, you see, I had to wrap it up. I had to have a killer and an
explanation. I hadn't counted on Dora Maunder—God rest her soul
—and I'd thought that Jonas, you know, would just, in time, go
away. But then things began to close in on me. I sent Mrs. Amos a
little note from Jonas telling her about his being a queer, and everything worked like a charm. She came into the agency like a thunder-
storm and people heard the poor fella weeping and carrying on the
afternoon before he—uh—took his life. Or . . ." green eyes vague
again, puzzled—"did he? Anyway, out the window with him."

Cane interrupted himself to get more coffee and dispose of two
hot buttered English muffins. Gus's throat wouldn't tolerate food,
but he swallowed a lot more coffee and went over to the table to mix
drinks.

"Jonas, man," he muttered over his shoulder. "*Jonas.*"

"Bit of a family matter," Cane said, looking slyly amused. "I believe your cousin Augustus Farnall is very big on the boards of two of
Homans' clients? Well, years ago, in New York, long before he knew
he would end up here, Ryan told Jonas something, over a bottle or
two or three."

Ryan had said, "Lord Augustus Farnall—he's chairman of the
board of Guardian Petroleum, you'll mind—Augustus Farnall and I
shared the favors of the same girl in New York at one time. Mistress,
I suppose *he'd* call her. He paid the rent, I got it for nothing." He
chuckled happily. "I knew about him. He never knew about me. It
was he in one door and I out the other, a regular farce. Anyway, he
married her. Not quite nine months afterward, she gave birth to a
boy. A jolly bouncing little redheaded broth of a boy."

"Yours?" Cane asked.

"I have every reason to believe so," Ryan said, sounding pleased with himself. "So has she." (Gus looked startled and then nodded. Except for the nose—good God, yes.) "She told Farnall she had a redheaded father. He's now the scion of the family. The only son. I'm told Farnall divorced his first wife because her production rate was zero. Or his—you never know about these things. Oh, the apple of his father's eye, Augustus the Third. Well, you can see, if that came out it could hardly be good for business, now could it? My business. Three-quarters of the billing snatched away at one fell swoop, and I with every penny I have in the world and a lot more in it, and I'm not exactly a young man. *I* don't hire anyone—by choice, anyway—over twenty-five. . . ."

Cane drank off half of his bloody mary, and went back to Ryan:

". . . Jonas thought it was a grand joke. He roared about it. On the strength of it he got himself a tremendous job with us and didn't have to turn a hand if he didn't feel like it. I was never quite happy with the arrangement. There was nothing to say that he wouldn't have it strike him funny again, sometime, someplace. . . ."

Ryan's eyes went strange again, distant, vague. "Jonas had a great sense of humor. Or has . . . sometimes a fella's not quite sure. . . . He found out, you know, a belly laugh on Aldington. Seems our conservative friend was a member of the Communist party when he was a freshman at Yale. Jonas was a Yalie himself and dug out a copy of a speech of Aldy's, very fiery, in the Yale Daily News. So what, it's a kid thing to do for a lot of people, but it tickled the hell out of Jonas. Now he'll never get to use it. Too bad. I'd like to have seen old Aldy's face. . . . Maybe I'll just mention it for kicks"—Ryan gave Cane an eerie conspiratorial grin—"at the trial."

Cane's eyes went hungrily to the table. "Any more English muffins? I hate to trouble you—thanks. You may be too shot, excuse the expression, to worry about the whys and wherefores, but of course Maunder came upon him in Trunk Street just after he'd patched up the windowpane. Is that apricot jam I see?"

He spread the second half of his muffin with preserves. "Ryan thought Shattner suspected what happened but he didn't want to rock the boat, he'd sunk everything he had in the agency too. He gets thanked for his silence by that note to his wife—Ryan wrote it—telling her he's a homosexual, probably with a lot of juicy details. Oh, and the car Maunder was so hot after—he parked it in a garage in Camden. Miss Rath's going to pick it up and drive it to a new home."

Gus refilled the beaded pewter mugs. He opened his mouth and Millie got there before him.

"That little boy. Is there any way he can't be destroyed?"

"I think we can shuffle that card to the bottom of the pack and keep it there, as far as the public goes," Cane said. "God knows there's enough else." He got his drink down quickly, preparing to leave, and then, rendered expansive by vodka, said, "I think you were perfectly safe all along, Miss Millie—except, like, if you went crazy—because killing you when you came looking for him might start people taking you seriously, your idea about him being shot over the phone, I mean."

From Gus, "Seriously, posthumously. Very helpful."

"You have a point." And then, awkwardly, "Now, about the body . . ."

Jonas was cremated the next morning. The service was short, smooth, and grim. Millie's father came down from Maine, and during a drink afterward with Millie and Gus and Olivia, while they all tried to huddle themselves back into life, into a resplendent day in June, Jerome Lester thoughtfully studied the sore-throated gray-eyed personable man sitting next to his daughter, across the table from him. Who had been at her side all through the dark ceremony, looking not at the long box and the door to its final slide but at Millie's face. A hand, an arm, supporting her, husbandly.

He left after the drink to catch his plane back to Maine. In a private aside, "Very nice man, Millie," he said. "I hope—but of course in any case you'll go your own way."

"I like your father," Gus said. "Interesting man. Tough. Takes a dim view, doesn't he?—But looked a little cheered up when he left us."

Olivia had gone, saying she hoped Olivia's Village was not in the hands of the receivers, and assured by Millie that everything Jonas had left behind, financially and otherwise—the grandfather clock and the cufflinks and the Bokhara—was naturally to go to his sister.

Millie, alone at the table with Gus, said, "Gus, I've been thinking—"

"Thinking what? Today is not a particularly good day for thinking."

"—now that you don't have to worry about me any more—perhaps it was some sort of Philadelphia fever?—we might separate for a week and find out if we still— And I have to see that man at CBS anyway, and there are things I have to attend to at the apartment— I don't want to force you into anything, just because—"

He gave her a long look.

"All right, Millie. Want to see Mike Garland? And decide who, really, suits you better?"

He kept looking. Bent head, hesitant thrush's voice. Lost again, a little. Doubting herself, blaming herself. Down somewhere with Jonas's ashes. Jonas, who thought he loved her, married her, and discarded her.

"No . . . although I'll have to tell him—"

"Tell him what?"

"That we can't—I mean—" She covered her face with her hands. "I'll make more sense tomorrow, maybe. Do you think you could get me a taxi to Thirtieth Street?"

He put her into the cab and lightly kissed her cheek.

"Good-bye, then, Millie. Have a nice trip home."

She sat and looked out of her second dirty wide window in a week while the train rocked and rushed on its way to New York.

The chattering of the tracks saying, Wel-come, Wel-come, Wel-come.

She was appalled at herself.

When she got off the train, she went up the escalator and turned immediately to a telephone booth and dialed.

"Gus?" she said. "You must forgive me. It was just—on top of all that awfulness—it seemed too much to expect . . . *you* . . . not only because of emergencies but for good. . . . Will you please, please, come here, again, to me?"

"I'd figured on the five o'clock, Millie," Gus said. "Now I think I can just—yes—catch the four."